WE LIKE IT CHERRY

JACY MORRIS

Cover designed by Alex Woodroe
Interior Illustrations by Blacky Shepherd
Edited by Alex Woodroe

Content warnings are available at the end of this book. Please consult this list for any particular subject matter you may be sensitive to.

WE LIKE IT CHERRY © 2025 by Jacy Morris

All rights reserved. No parts of this publication may be reproduced, distributed or transmitted in any form by any means, except for brief excerpts for the purpose of review, without the prior written consent of the owner. All inquiries should be addressed to tenebrouspress@gmail.com.

Published by Tenebrous Press.
   Visit our website at www.tenebrouspress.com.

First Printing, August 2025.

The characters and events portrayed in this work are fictitious. Any similarity to real persons, living or dead, is coincidental and not intended by the author.

Print ISBN: 978-1-959790-33-4
eBook ISBN: 978-1-959790-34-1

Cover designed by Alex Woodroe.

Interior illustrations by Blacky Shepherd.

Edited by Alex Woodroe.

Formatting by Lori Michelle.

All creators in this publication have signed an AI-free agreement. To the best of our knowledge, this publication is free from machine-generated content

Also by Jacy Morris:

Bury My Heart with a Keyboard (A Collection)
The Drop
One Night Stand at the End of the World
One-Shot
The Taxidermied Man
This Rotten World

Selected Works from Tenebrous Press:

Puppet's Banquet
by Valkyrie Loughcrewe

Casual
a novel by Koji A. Dae

All Your Friends are Here
stories by M.Shaw

TRVE CVLT
a novel by Michael Bettendorf

A Spectre is Haunting Greentree
a novel by Carson Winter

From the Belly
a novel by Emmett Nahil

Posthaste Manor
a novel by Jolie Toomajan & Carson Winter

Dehiscent
a novella by Ashley Deng

More titles at www.TenebrousPress.com

THE START OF A TRADITION

WHITE ICE BLINDED the man. Though large, he seemed small on the glacial sheet. In his beard, frost had collected, the moisture from his lungs expelled through cracked and bleeding lips.

He ran hard, his eyes squinting against the sun's reflection off the ice—a beautiful day.

Tagak admired the man, liked the way the exposed portions of his skin had turned pink like the char when they returned home to spawn in the spring—the color of a new beginning, the color of the cycle of life.

The man stumbled on the sheet, tumbling to the ice. The ancestors watched.

Kikkik waved him on, but Tagak held Kikkik back.

"It is good for him to work. Makes the meat richer."

Kikkik nodded. Knew he was right. The hunter wasn't known for his patience. Kikkik wasn't known for much, really.

The pink men had appeared out of nowhere, landing on the eastern ridge of the bay, at the edge of the glacier where the ancestors lived, and materialized out of early morning fog in the strangest boat to ever glide upon the water of the bay. When Tagak had joined the elder's greeting party, they had gone armed, for the people were unlike anyone they had ever seen. Not only were they tall, but their skin was sickly, lacked the right color, as if they had been frozen, or as if they had fallen over the side of an umiak, lived underwater for a few months, and then washed up on shore with their skin bleached by the thirsty waters.

At first, Tagak had thought these were ancient ancestors returned from the dead, but when the elder spoke to them, they seemed confused, spoke words back no one understood. The ancestors would never forget their language.

The strangers wore weapons on their hips, sharp things made from a material the Winoquin—the People—were unfamiliar with. Their blades reflected the sun like the ice, and they smiled and laughed.

It wasn't long before they all sat down to dinner, trying to figure out each other's ways using hand gestures to communicate. Though they could not understand each other's words, they all spoke the language of food. Seated around whale flesh and seal meat, a cache of tubers they'd been saving for the dark times, when the sun never came up, when the ancestors played in the sky as shifting green light, they squatted in the clearing between their ice homes and feasted. With their bare hands, they tore chunks from the carcasses and brought their blood-soaked hands to their mouths. Together, the two peoples fed and smiled and laughed.

As the never-ending day stretched onward, the spirits of their unborn ancestors dancing as clouds in the sky, the pale men grew rough, demanding, started pawing at the women. Kikkik didn't care for this, insisted these men were lost, demons from a dark place. They had no souls, no spirits, no names, and that's why their skin was pale and their eyes even paler. They didn't belong, were a travesty.

This he said in the circle with the pale men listening, and no one argued with him. When one of them tore the clothes from the elder's daughter, the Winoquin stood, spears in hand, waved the men away.

The demons stood tall and proud, towering over them, dressed in furs of animals the Winoquin had never seen before. Their hands dropped to their hips, and Kikkik sent a spear through one of the men. His aim was true, stole the breath right out of the dying man's lungs, and the man fell over on his side.

The other men scattered, their lust and hunger forgotten as one of their own lay on the ground, turning the snow red.

Tagak followed Kikkik, chasing after the man who had started it all. Instead of heading toward his ship, the man, his blood in his loins instead of his brains, took off running across the glacier. They chased him; Kikkik carrying his spear, Tagak wielding a harpoon.

"They're demons," Kikkik said.

Tagak didn't know one way or another, but he figured if you were going to start something, you'd better finish it. They chased

WE LIKE IT CHERRY

the pale man, laughing and hollering. With only his weapon on his hip, he was no match for them, despite his larger size.

He shuffled quickly across the white sheet, the clouds above mocking him.

After a great sprint, he fell to the ice, his energy drained. Tagak and Kikkik stood over him.

Without a word, Tagak threw his harpoon through the man's belly. Lying on his back, his hands trying to keep his blood inside, Kikkik moved in, stabbing the man in the throat with his spear. They did this quickly, efficiently, for there was no sense in taking pleasure in another man's death. It had to be done sometimes . . . sometimes.

Tagak fashioned a rope to the end of the harpoon, and using this, they dragged the violator back to their village. In a week they'd move on, migrating as the season changed. But for now, the village was Home.

Back in the village, they found the other pale men had fled, taken their boat and sailed away on the cold sea. They could just make out the squares of their sails as they drifted away, the ancestors' breath pushing them onto the next world. Next time, the Winoquin would kill them as soon as they saw them.

"We must eat them," said Kikkik, "devour their evil so it may never affect us again."

The elder nodded, and the Winoquin set about preparing the tall men, the giants, peeling off their skin and chucking it into the sea for the fish and gods to nibble. When the pale men were as red as a cherry, they chopped into their flesh with their stone blades, brought the men to their lips in chunks where they kissed them before slipping them into their mouths and chewing them to nothing.

And that year, out of all the years, their hunting was the best. Blessed by the spirits for their good deed, their numbers grew, the caribou ran in packs, and the seals were plentiful. A tradition was born.

CHAPTER 1
EYES ARE LIES, MY BOY

NOTHING NEW. Nothing new. He'd seen it all before. The same traditions, not even real traditions, for this tribe. Made-up, borrowed, embellished—stolen in other words. It had to be that way though. What were you to do when your traditions had been buried underneath the bootheel of the American government, when they couldn't be passed on because your children had been sent off to boarding schools to be whitewashed?

You had to have something of your own to say, "This is who we are. We're not like them. We're different—and these traditions, though they were never ours, show that." Dressed like the Plains Tribes, the residents of this reservation in the Pacific Northwest, danced to music their ancestors had never played, wearing clothes their ancestors had never worn, performing rituals the tribe had never practiced.

But you had to have something.

What could you do when you didn't know who you were? When you knew everything that had made your tribe what it was had been scattered to the four winds?

Ezra Montbanc's thoughts ran dark today. But no one would know. He wouldn't let the mask slip, had to wear it, just as these Indians paraded around their parade grounds wearing their masks and face paint, he had his own.

"Today, the Ranutni are celebrating their special day. Three days of celebration, three days on the powwow grounds."

Ezra held a small microphone in his brown hands. It didn't do anything, was purely for show, and made him seem more official. The real microphone was powered by a battery pack stuffed in his back pocket, a wire snaking up his "I'm not as white as you think I am" T-shirt, and ending in a barely visible microphone hanging off his shirt collar.

He'd been to dozens of celebrations like this, seen them across the country. All the same, all homogenized despite the thousands of different cultures of the Indigenous peoples of America . . . all pressed together like Spam, all salty . . . all predictable.

As Stu Nofire locked in on Ezra with the camera, Ezra had to admit he was bored.

At first, it had been fun traveling around the U.S., taking in the culture, reveling in it. It made him feel more . . . Native, like not so much of a faker, but now that he'd seen it all, realized it was all the same, he found it did the opposite, made him feel like a tourist among the people with whom he shared blood. *How can they pretend like this?*

But still he smiled, still he delivered the lines as he interviewed the powwow princess, the powwow prince. He smiled at the children, for real, at least, perhaps the only real thing he did. He ate fry bread, the same damn recipe, the same damn taste as all the fry bread he'd eaten on a hundred different parade grounds.

If he never ate another piece of fry bread, it would be too soon.

On and on he went, the fire rising in the night, the dancers spinning in place, moving within a circle, circles within circles. The thing about a circle—it doesn't fucking go anywhere.

Ezra and Stu had been working for the Expose Channel for years, filling up a block on Tuesday mornings with their ethnic-themed series, documenting the celebrations of Indigenous communities across Canada and the United States. Their show didn't make much money, didn't pull investors because everyone knew Natives didn't have money to spend, and no one else watched the thing. The show seemed to exist solely as a tax write-off for the network, and as a badge on their chest, the word "Diversity" etched within the proverbial bronze star.

He was tired of it. Tired of feeling useless. Nothing he did was new; nothing he did was *journalism*, the subject he'd attended college for. He was a hack, a no-talent nothing, toiling on this hamster wheel of a show.

After the Grand Entry, Ezra and Stu packed up the camera equipment, adjourned to their tent, and sat inside.

WE LIKE IT CHERRY

Stu turned on the lantern, dim so it wouldn't cast their shadows on the side of the tent. Ezra reached into his bag, pulled out a bottle of vodka, unscrewed the top and took a healthy swig. It tasted like gasoline, went down hard.

Stu held out his hand, and together, they sat sipping in the dark.

"You know, powwows wouldn't be so bad if they just let you drink," said Ezra, for the hundredth time.

Stu scoffed. "Get a bunch of Injuns all fired up, and then fill 'em with the old firewater, and you know what you have—a fucking brawl instead of a powwow. Mamas and grandmamas crawling all over the parade grounds crying for their lost loved ones. No one wants that."

"Maybe I do," Ezra said. "That'd be something at least. But no, they just go on—well, pass the fucking bottle, chief."

The fans of their show, maybe a thousand of them, would be surprised to find Ezra talking in this manner, would be surprised to see him getting drunk in a tent at an event that declared itself "alcohol and drug free." But what were a thousand fans in the grand scheme of things? If only he could do what he'd been born to do—go out and find an actual story, not rehash this shit that had been rehashed already, a dozen times in season one, ten times in season two and three, and now eight times in season four. He doubted there would be a fifth season. He stood on the precipice of anonymity; knew he was on the way out.

When they were good and buzzed, Ezra turned down the light, and they stripped off their clothes and drunk fucked until two in the morning.

When Stu rolled over on his side in the middle of the night, Ezra awoke. Needing to take a piss, Ezra fumbled around for his clothing, managed to find his pants with the pack of cigarettes in the pockets, and stepped out into the cool night.

Fog hung over the camping area, chilly and white. The cones of teepees, never a thing for the ancient Ranutni, jutted up into the sky like nipples.

He wandered to the edge of the campground, shirtless, shoeless, like a real Indian. A few people sat up staring into campfires, the flames flickering off their faces. He liked Native American faces at night, especially in firelight, found they all looked like soothsayers and oracles. Pony up to any one of these coal-glaring founts of wisdom, and you could fix your life in a matter of minutes. At least, that's what he liked to think.

Ezra stood at the edge of a forest pissing, staring up at the thick trees, their branches all encompassing. They shot up into the air like arrows waiting to take flight. He zipped his pants and fished in his pocket. Underneath one of these massive fir trees—he didn't know its species—he wasn't that type of Indian—he lit a cigarette, scanned around for the powwow police to come and escort him from the premises, which would be fine by him. Maybe he and Stu could drive to the coast, check out a brewery or something.

There you go. That's the ticket. I should be touring the country checking out breweries. That would be something, anything. Even if a brewery sucked or felt familiar, at least you could get wrecked and film your damn show.

A voice coughed in the darkness, and Ezra dropped the cigarette to the ground while blowing smoke out of his mouth. With his bare foot, he stomped on the thing, burning his sole, as he waved his hand in the air to dissipate the smoke.

"You don't have to hide on my account," the voice said.

The accent was strange, unfamiliar, unplaceable. The shadow that emerged from the forest was small, at least half a foot shorter than Ezra, who was of average height.

"Who's there?" Ezra asked, still waving his hand through the cloud of smoke hanging on the foggy air.

The shape appeared, but he couldn't make out its features.

"You're the TV man," the voice said.

"I guess so."

"You came by my booth today."

Ezra had walked by every booth—all the same, hand-crafted bits and bobs for the tourists to take home, dreamcatchers made by people whose only dream was to make a little money.

"I sell whale-bone carvings," the short shadow prompted.

"Oh, yeah," he said, the man's face coming back to him. It was an ugly thing, wrinkled and pinched, old before its time. His fingers were stubby and thick, maybe due to all the carving. "Say, that's not real whale bone, is it?"

At this, the man seemed to hitch, his mouth dropping open for a second.

WE LIKE IT CHERRY

"I mean it can't be real, right? They're not going to let whale bone across the border. You're from Canada, right?"

"It is whale bone," the man insisted. "And no, they don't let whale bone across the border. But if you tell 'em it's polished driftwood, they don't know the difference."

Ezra nodded his head. *Anything for a buck.*

"You're the host of that show, aren't you?"

That show. No one ever remembered its name. Once it was off the air, no one would remember it had existed at all. It would vanish as if it had never been real, and Ezra along with it. "Yeah. Indigenous Insider, that's me."

"Are you proud of what you do?"

"As proud as anyone can be, I suppose."

The man nodded in the gloom. "I see."

"How can you see anything in this dark?"

"The dark is the best time to see things. Eyes are lies, my boy. Eyes are lies. Take them away and the truth is revealed. We know who we are in the darkness. We reveal our secrets to ourselves and to others. I see yours now."

Goddamn. It never fails. Walk around a powwow at night, and you always run into some motherfucker like this, wandering around, looking to shoot his wisdom all over you in the pitch black. "What secrets?" he asked, just to humor the man.

"You want to do more. You want to do something that matters."

Ezra's breath caught in his throat. Then he shook his head. A bunch of bullshit. "Doesn't everybody?"

"No, some people are happy with their lives."

"Are you happy?"

"Oh, sure. I'd like to show you my happiness."

"If you're hitting on me, I'm not interested."

The man laughed, a hoarse thing, the sound of someone who lived in a house where a fire was always going. "My happiness is a place."

"What place?"

"My home, my land. You should go. Do your show there."

"Where?"

"Baffin Island."

Ezra wasn't an atlas, had no idea where anything was outside the United States. "Where's that?"

"North," the man said.
"Canada?"
"No. Norther than that."
Ezra nodded, got the picture.
"What would I see if I went there?" he asked, curious despite himself.
"A different world."
They fell silent, and the silence grew awkward. Ezra's brain, fuzzy with alcohol, struggled to manufacture some way out of the conversation, some way to escape this earnest bumpkin who was so proud of his shitty home, a pile of rocks next to a bunch of frozen water.
"There's a festival soon; the conditions are right."
"What festival?"
"It doesn't have a name. It just is."
"And what do you do at this ceremony."
"I don't know. I've never been."
Ezra was sure he was being fucked with. "Come on, man. It's too late for this shit."
"It's a festival from the old times. When the conditions are right, we have it. Conditions haven't been right in my lifetime, but this year, they are."
"What conditions?"
"Go. You'll see. Bring your show."
They talked for a little longer, exchanging information. Then Ezra returned to his lover, his partner, crawled in behind him, and fell asleep.

CHAPTER 2
THE CREW

THE WINOQUIN LIVED beyond the imaginary dotted line of the Arctic Circle, an isolated environment, prone to killing those who did not know the ways of the land. Forget booking a Delta flight to the Winoquin homeland, because no runways existed for a plane to land. You couldn't drive there; there were no roads. The only way to reach the lone outpost of this most nomadic of people was by boat, or by walking hundreds of miles across the temporarily revealed arctic scrublands, hopefully avoiding the bears and the wolves that sometimes ranged north in the summer to avoid man.

You had to fly into the Arctic Bay Airport, populated by Inuit workers and white people who existed on the fringes of society. From there, you had to charter a fishing trawler. Thankfully, Ezra, Stu, and the other two people on their production team traveled in the summer. In the winter, only an icebreaker could navigate the frozen water surrounding Baffin Island. Although, if it was the winter, they could have taken a dog sled across the northern tip of the semi-phallic landmass.

But it was July, and the daytime sun, flat and hard, without the typical glare one might experience in the more temperate regions of North America, kept the land cooking at a steamy fifty-degrees Fahrenheit. On the boat, the cold air clinging to the slate-blue waters made it feel much chillier.

Ezra rode at the bow, the rest of the crew sheltering within the captain's cabin. For this adventure, the Expose Network had ponied up some cash, once the network's research team realized how isolated and unknown the Winoquin were. Often confused with the Inuit who lived in the same area, the two tribes would have nothing to do with each other, wouldn't even be in the same place. No one could say why. It was an old taboo, its genesis buried in the forgotten past.

DNA evidence had shown no genetic connection between the two groups of people, despite similarities in appearance and culture. The Winoquin were quite simply their own thing. Few, if any, ever left the small village permanently. Many left temporarily, went out in the world to see what it was like, sometimes bringing back things they liked, machinery, ideas.

Other than that, little else was known about the mysterious tribe, though they were as open and kind as any tribe according to those who had dared adventure to the edge of the frozen world to get to know them.

Maybe they're just boring?

Ezra hoped not. In his heart, he kept hoping this was the break, this was the one that would transform him from a dude who went to powwows and into an actual, story-breaking journalist. He stood at the bow of the ship, Leonardo Dicaprio-ing, watching the world sail by.

"Come away from there," Stu called.

"It's fine!" Ezra shouted back.

"Yeah, until you get washed into that water. The captain says you might last for five minutes before you started suffering from hypothermia."

As if to punctuate Stu's warning, the tip of the ship bowed down, sliced through a swelling wall of water, and sprayed both Ezra and Stu with the iciest spray of ocean they had ever felt.

Ezra gasped and slipped, his hand going to the railing to prevent him from sliding overboard. Stu, on the other hand, went down on the deck, sliding and crashing against the side of the boat.

Ezra scrambled free of the ship's prow, made it to Stu's side on shaky legs, and helped him to his feet.

"Seems to be getting a bit rougher," Stu said.

"I like it rough," Ezra hinted.

"Pervert," Stu said, smiling at Ezra. Stu brushed at his jacket with gloved hands, wiping as much frigid water off his coat as he could manage. "Fuck, I'm cold."

Together, the two went below deck, walking like drunks as the boat bobbed up and down.

WE LIKE IT CHERRY

The captain's quarters were not spacious by any stretch of the imagination. In fact, they were downright claustrophobic. On the wall hung all sorts of paraphernalia Ezra supposed one would need if they were making their life at sea, nets, fishing poles, floats, a harpoon, all covered in a layer of dried ocean scum. As the ship dipped up and down, Ezra rubbed his hands together, held them out to the heater.

Their sound man, Jonesy, couldn't help but laugh at them as Ezra and Stu tried to warm up. "I hate to break it to ya, but this is about as warm as you're gonna be for the next week."

Seven days in this cold place, and not a tree in sight. Just cold ocean and gray and green grasses, the occasional bush every now and then. What a weird place for humans to live. You could have given Ezra all the money in the world, and he wouldn't live in this part of the world.

"Keep laughing, Jonesy. We'll see how you like it when you're standing out there with your boom in the air."

Jonesy scoffed and waved Ezra away. "I come prepared for the job. You two act like you've never been in cold weather before."

The cantankerous sound man, weighing two bills plus some, most of it from his beer belly, had a point.

"Layers, gentlemen," their producer Scott said.

Scott was a plain sort of man, brown hair, a smugness to his lips, the type of dude that only listened to music on vinyl, and only if it was older than he was. Not so bad as a producer, but as an actual person, he left a little to be desired. He didn't have a fun bone in his body.

"Check it out," Scott said. He stood up, undid his loose outer parka, revealed another parka underneath. "The outer layer prevents the wind from getting in. The layer underneath traps your body heat, keeping you warm. Might want to see if you can trade for another jacket when we get to town."

Scott always knew everything, had been a producer on several National Geographic programs. In Scott's mind, this made him worldly and wise. In Ezra's mind, it made him a pain-in-the-ass know-it-all, but he was the network's mouthpiece, sent along because Stu and Ezra were out of their element. Scott was a modern-day adventurer. While he had trouble getting along with his own crew, put him in a land with complete strangers and a foreign culture, and he'd shine—a handy person to have along, if a bit annoying.

"You think they got a bar in this place?" Ezra asked.

"If they do, I doubt you'll want to drink any of it. Probably homemade seal wine or something like that," Jonesy said.

Scott chimed in, because he always did. He couldn't help it. "From the accounts I've read, the Winoquin don't allow alcohol in their community."

"Weed?" Stu asked.

"Nope. As far as I can tell, the only stimulants you might find are going to be tobacco and coffee."

"Oh, God, at least we can have coffee," Stu said.

"And cigarettes," Ezra added.

Stu didn't like that Ezra smoked, but it was who he was. Maybe one day he'd quit, when he thought there was a future to live for.

"What else do you know about the Winoquin?" Ezra asked, already regretting the question, as it would most likely lead to an hour-long presentation on the subject from Scott, but hell, they had some time to kill.

"Not much to know. Hunter-gatherer culture, mostly nomadic. Speak a language with a bunch of k's and t's and other sounds you and I can't hope to make. They're virtually unchanged. It's like when they discover a new tribe in the Amazon, only this one has always been hiding in plain sight."

"Well, that was thankfully brief," Stu added.

Scott shot him that producer look. All producers had it, that look that said, "Listen, enough with the jocularity. I'm not here to be your friend. I'm here to get the job done and make some money in the process."

They had seen a lot of Scott at the beginning of Indigenous Insider, when Stu, Jonesy, and Ezra had all been getting their feet wet. Now that they knew the ropes, they didn't really need Scott around. But this was a new location, which would offer new challenges, and Scott could get the job done if something came about. He was, even though Ezra hated to admit it, wise and worldly in a way Stu and Ezra could never hope to be.

Jonesy, on the other hand, was the complete opposite of worldly. He carried his vices with him wherever he went, expected others to cater to them. He was the type of ugly American people

WE LIKE IT CHERRY

in foreign countries complained about. The guy who went to a place, got wasted as fuck, and then started flashing cash about when he had an urge.

"You think there's like . . . Winoquin pussy to be had?" Jonesy asked.

"Jesus, dude," Stu said.

"What?" Jonesy asked, his hands held palm up, as if he couldn't help himself.

"Have some fucking class," Ezra said.

"Psshh," Jonesy hissed, dismissing the two with a wave of his hands. "It's a legitimate question. Just because you two aren't interested, doesn't mean I'm not."

Jonesy's boorish remark sparked a question in Ezra's mind. "Do they have gay people in this place?"

"Beats me," Scott said. "Couldn't find much on cultural rituals and mores, mostly stuff about families and sticking together."

"Are they all like inbred and shit?" Jonesy asked.

Ezra couldn't wait to get off the boat and start filming. At least then Jonesy would have to shut the fuck up. Say what you would about his blue-collar, muff-diver reputation, but he got the job done, and could keep quiet when he needed to.

Scott shrugged, "Well, I didn't run a DNA diagnostic on them, but I think it's safe to assume some of that is going on."

"I don't know," Ezra said. "Maq didn't seem so strange to me. Seemed pretty normal, although he was on the small side."

"Well, whatever happens, just don't say anything about it," Stu said.

"You don't have to tell me. I'm not the one who goes around putting my foot in my mouth ten times a day," Ezra said, hiking a thumb in Jonesy's direction.

In mock outrage, Jonesy's eyes went wide and in a defensive tone, he said, "Fuck you two. You know I'm as professional as they come."

Ezra rolled his eyes as he rubbed his hands together trying to get the feeling back in his fingertips.

Two hours later, they climbed in a dinghy, and the ship's first and only mate rowed them ashore.

CHAPTER 3
SENTIENT SUSHI

MAQ WAITED FOR them on the beach, a shelf of cold rocks rising out of the water. As the dinghy ground to shore, he walked out to the water's edge, waded in, and pulled the boat aground, splashing through the freezing water as Ezra might glide through a pool in Vegas to order himself another drink at the poolside bar. Together, Ezra and Stu climbed out, hauling their gear, which mostly consisted of changes of clothes and Stu's camera equipment.

Maq held out his wet hand and said, "Welcome to the village."

Stu, once more on solid ground, appeared to fight a wave of nausea as the world went still around him. A chill wind swept across the water and battered him around his ears. He scanned the beachside, looking for any signs of a village, but he saw nothing.

"If you say so," Ezra said.

Stu, ever the professional, dragged his gear up the beach, away from the water, and then undid the latches on the hardcase for his camera. He pulled it out, fiddled with it a bit, and then began recording. He would be like that for the rest of the day, until bedtime, the camera glued to his face as he recorded anything and everything, only stopping to swap out storage drives and batteries. Another box, filled with charged batteries and more storage drives, sat untouched. For a week's worth of filming, they had brought several hundred thousand dollars of equipment.

Stu got the camera up and running while Ezra set up his own microphone. The howl of the ocean wind would most likely wind up marring the sound tracks but there was nothing to do about it.

WE LIKE IT CHERRY

They might be able to filter it out in post, but he doubted it; the wind was too strong, roaring off the bay.

When they were ready, Ezra began performing. "Ho, Maq. Thanks for having us!"

Maq turned and looked at the camera out of the corner of his eye.

"Don't look at the camera, Maq. Look at me."

The affable Maq went wooden then. It happened sometimes. But the more he was around the camera, the more accustomed he'd get. Hopefully, or else they weren't going to be able to use any of his shit.

The man stood robed in an ancient, tan parka. Underneath this parka, Ezra saw the faded blue of another underneath. *Did everyone know about the layering thing?*

"Let me ask you something, Maq. We're out here, at the end of the world ostensibly, because this is where you live. What is the name of this place, you know, so the folks back home can Google Earth it."

Maq shrugged, his jackets rasping against each other. "No name," Maq said.

"What do you call it?"

"Home?" he asked, scratching his head.

"How long has it been home?"

"You'd have to ask the elder, but a long time."

Stu gave him the thumbs-up, stopped recording.

In the meantime, they stood on the edge of the coast, watching as the first mate started rowing the dinghy back out to sea. On the deck of the boat, Jonesy and Scott bobbed up and down as they waited patiently for their ride.

The wind howling off the water cut right through his jacket. "Jesus," he managed to hiss, before the stiff breeze stole his breath away.

Having nothing else better to do, he asked Maq, "You mind if I smoke?"

Maq shook his head. "It is not our way to tell others what they can and can't do, as long as it doesn't hurt the community."

That was good enough for Ezra. He pulled a cigarette free, lit it, and watched as the breeze snatched the smoke from his mouth, sent it hurtling across a gently sloping land covered in autumnal looking grasses.

The biting wind kept the cherry of his cigarette pointed and glowing red, and he watched as the ash fluttered from the end, spiraling and spinning away to nowhere.

Their presence hadn't gone unnoticed, and as he watched, people appeared from low huts that blended in with the environment, their roofs cleverly hidden by chunks of sod with more of those orange and faded-green grasses growing out of them. They came in twos and threes, smiles on their faces, their teeth white and perfect, unmarred by things like sugar or processed foods. Their eyes were slits in their skulls, all but for the children who hadn't yet been conditioned to squint against this world's harsh glare. Wide-eyed, fresh, they came with a look of awe on their faces, and Ezra prepared himself for the poking and prodding that comes when people so unused to seeing anyone but their family appeared out of nowhere, as if by magic.

He was familiar with it. In some of the smaller, more out of the way reservations he'd visited, the children were like that, their world turned on its head by the mere presence of someone new.

At the back of the pack, an old man tottered, walking with the support of a bleached piece of wood. No one aided him or dishonored him by offering help. He strode hunched but proud across the grasses, his feet bound in thick moccasins made of hide and stitched with dried guts to make thread.

Maq stood to the side, his head bowed, and Ezra, suddenly realizing his cigarette still smoldered in his hand, looked for someplace to drop it. Eventually, he bent down, brushed it out against a rock, leaving a dark, charcoal smudge on the stone. He threw the burned butt into his pack of smokes, though he knew it would make all the other cigarettes reek like stale smoke.

When Ezra tossed a look over his shoulder, he spotted Jonesy and Scott about halfway across the water.

The group gathered around him, the children clutching their mothers' thick skirts, peering around their hips at Ezra and Stu.

Stu, never one to miss an opportunity, brought his camera up to his eye, began filming.

The old man spoke, a lispy language, clicks and sibilance in equal measure.

Maq translated for him. "He welcomes you," he said. "You bring the Winoquin great honor with your presence."

WE LIKE IT CHERRY

Ezra nodded, then said, "Thank you for inviting us. It is our honor to take part in your celebration."

The old man looked to Maq, waited for the translation. He nodded when Maq finished, spoke again, his thin, cracked lips barely moving as he spoke.

"Maq will show you our village, and then you will come to our fire, and we will feast together," Maq translated.

"I will be honored," Ezra said. "Thank you for your hospitality."

Maq made the sounds of the Winoquin language, and the old man nodded, tapped his throat at Ezra.

"Now you tap," Maq said.

Ezra mimicked the man's movements, and then the old man began his slow trundle back to the village.

The women, children, and men of the Winoquin tribe didn't depart, however. They clung to Ezra and the others like summer gnats, whispering and saying things Ezra couldn't understand.

When Jonesy and Scott reached the shore, Ezra and Stu helped them unload and filled them in on what had happened so far.

"Right," Scott said. "Let's take this tour and then get some food. I'm starving."

Scott's eyes glowed with the promise of adventure, of experiences new and novel, but Ezra didn't share the same sentiment. He didn't know what they ate out here, probably a bunch of fish, weird things from underneath rocks, but he doubted he would find anything appetizing.

"Follow me," Maq said. "We'll set your things in the village."

"Will it be safe?" Stu asked, ever-protective of the expensive equipment. It was all insured, but the higher-ups at the network got pissed when you had to actually make a claim on that insurance.

"No one will touch your things without permission," Maq said.

They lugged the hardcases across the rocky shore, the land sloping gently upward from the beach.

"Watch out for her," Maq said.

"Her? Who?" Ezra asked.

Maq pointed at a small cairn of rocks.

"Is that a grave?" Ezra asked.

Behind him, Scott stood with his ever-present clipboard in his hand, jotting down notes for the story editors to save them time, so they could cobble something coherent out of a week's worth of footage, much of it pointless.

Maq nodded. "The ground is too rocky to dig deep, so we dig a little way, cover them in rocks so the birds don't get them. That's Harkisi. She loved the beach, it's a good place for her to be. She will be born soon again."

"Born soon?"

"When one is born, another is reborn."

"Reincarnation?"

Maq shrugged, didn't quite get what Ezra was asking.

They walked onward, placing their gear in the middle of the village. The children, though curious, did not rush to inspect the boxes as the children of reservations past had done. They kept a respectful distance.

The tour of Home didn't take as long as Ezra would have expected. There wasn't much to see, after all.

As far as structures went, there was only one structure Ezra would have recognized, a small shed, made of bleached, ancient wood. When the door opened, they were assaulted by the smell of rotting meat and flesh.

"This is where we cure hides and smoke fish to help us through the winter months," Maq said.

Ezra poked his head inside, resisting the urge to cover his nose with his hand. Inside, he spied a variety of racks, a hole cut in the roof, and a smoldering fire. A soot-stained man, naked to his waist, waved at Ezra before tossing another handful of dried grass on the fire.

As Ezra backed out, Stu swooped in, collecting footage.

From there, Maq took them around the village, pointing out different cairns, talking about the people buried underneath as if they were merely taking a nap.

He pointed to the south, spoke of Baffin Island, pointed to the west, spoke of the towns in the distance, he pointed to the east, spoke of the big ocean, the place where the lost, those who succumbed to the gray mind, went when they died. Then he turned north, and a smile spread across his face. "There is the place where we go tomorrow. Tolby Island. It is a sacred place to us."

"What is so sacred about it?"

"Why is the sun the sun?"

WE LIKE IT CHERRY

Ezra couldn't argue with questions like that.

"If it's so sacred, why don't you live over there?"

"If we stay, we use up all the magic, or the magic uses us all up. Either way is no good. Too much of a good thing, yeah?"

Ezra nodded. One cigarette after a long day was a glorious thing. Ten cigarettes after a long day, less so. One beer after a long day, exquisite. Twelve beers . . . regret.

Back in the community circle, nestled between all the camouflaged huts, Maq pointed them to the room they'd be staying in. It was small; the roof so low they all had to duck when they went in. It smelled of earth and smoke. A small room at the back lay lowered in the ground, sealskin blankets arranged around a low table made of driftwood. On top of this driftwood rested an oil lamp. A wick lying on the lamp's edge burned slowly and steadily.

Maq, understanding inherently that they had never seen such a device, showed them how it worked. The wick had to continually be monitored, or it would start to smoke. Above the flame hung a flap of whale blubber, that, when heated by the flame, would drip more fat into the oil lamp's reservoir. The lamp itself was made of rough, green stone, shaped into a crescent moon shape. The light it gave off was pleasant and the smell faintly gamy but not too strong.

When they understood how the lamp worked, and all their gear was stowed, with the exception of the stuff they were using, they exited the small hut, ducking low so as not to bump their heads.

Outside, it was as bright as it had been several hours ago. Too bright for nine in the evening.

"Does it get any darker?" Ezra asked.

Maq smiled. "Nope, you can work on your tan all day."

The humor was welcome. For a while there, Ezra had started to feel like a burden to poor Maq, apparently the only person who could speak English in the village.

"How did you learn English?" asked Ezra as they stalked over well-worn grasses to the communal firepit.

"I was needed. The elder called on me, so I went to the schools, learned the languages. English, French."

"Did you like school?"

Maq looked at Ezra as if he were crazy. "Does anyone like school? It's a bad place, despite the good they try to do. Man isn't made to be this way, children even less so. Sitting at a desk, inside, locked away from the world around you. It's no wonder the lands down below are in such trouble."

Maq seemed like he was going to say more, but then his eyes shifted to the camera in Stu's hands, and he clammed up, aware he was being recorded once more.

Dammit. And he was just about to say some cool shit, too. Internally, Ezra shrugged, knew there would be more time. Scott scribbled in his notebook, and Ezra could feel the threads of this story coming together. That was the key to making a good documentary—the threads of a story. You didn't just go and film shit and then play it for people. You had to tailor it, had to spell it out for the masses, wrap it up in a tiny little bow at the end. You had to find the thread early, so you could pull on it, unravel the people and their culture so the audience could feel it, experience it without ever leaving their couch.

That's what made people like Anthony Bourdain so special. Motherfucker just traveled around the world drinking beers and smoking cigarettes, and he was able to make meaning from all these random events, all the random meals and encounters, and then tie it all together with a twist of poetic philosophy at the end of the damn show.

Ezra was trying to do that, to emulate his idol, but it was hard when he was only given so much to work with. So far, their visit with the Winoquin had felt about as exciting as a visit to the DMV, but there was something there in Maq, something he'd almost said that sparked some interest in Ezra. Maybe he was only trying to read into it, trying to see something when there was nothing, but if it kept him interested, more power to him. He would pull the thread, slowly at first, and then once he got the hang of it, he would tug, yank the story out of Maq one way or another.

At the fire, Ezra and the crew gathered around, sitting on blankets among the other villagers. Altogether, there were maybe fifty people present, many of them children. The women were stout and as hardy as the men.

"Is this everyone in your tribe?" Ezra asked.

Maq looked up, relayed the question to the elder, and then spoke in English. "This isn't everyone. Many of the men are away, preparing for the celebration."

WE LIKE IT CHERRY

"Where?" Ezra asked, hoping to get a preview of what was to come.

Maq smiled. "You'll see."

The women bustled around the fire, spearing chunks of fish through the middle with sharpened sticks which they placed on a spit. Juices fell from the meat as they turned them over the fire.

"What do we have here?" Ezra asked.

"Here we have arctic char. This is like . . . our bread."

"How big do they get?" Ezra asked.

Maq held his hands apart, about two feet. "Good meat. Good eat."

Ezra nodded. From there, he fell into the type of trance they would always show on the show, just video of him staring into the fire. Back in the studio in L.A., they would throw him in the room with a story producer and come up with some folksy, introspective bullshit to lay over top of the imagery. Those scenes gave him an excuse to stare into the flames and fall silent, and Ezra didn't mind one bit. The people around him didn't usually mind either, and no one here was different.

While they waited for the food to cook, the children played games off to the side. They would stand across from each other, leap straight into the air, and kick their legs, as if trying to kick their own faces. A third person judged their height, the winners celebrating and the losers walking away, anxious to try again. Round after round they went, leaping into the air, smiles plastered to their innocent faces. They didn't know of school, didn't know of Spider-Man, didn't know of drugs and homelessness. A perfect life for them. For a second, Ezra almost envied them, and then a cold wind slapped him across the cheek.

Stu moved in a circle, scoring footage of faces and flames, no doubt wondering if he was going to have to eat meat. A staunch vegetarian, Stu only ever compromised his values in situations like this.When the char had charred, the elder waved him over. He nodded at Ezra, the smell of roasting meat meeting his nose. Now it was time for his orgasm moment, to pretend like the food he was eating was the best shit he'd ever had. Television chefs over the years had been practicing this technique for years, popping chunks of steaming food in their mouths and then squeezing their eyes shut, pretending like they were popping off in someone as they chewed. With confident fingers, Ezra reached out to the steaming spit of fish. He pulled with his fingers, knowing there would be no silverware here, only hands covered in grease going from meat to mouth.

Maq nodded at him, assured him he wasn't breaking any cultural taboos, and then he brought the steaming nugget of meat to his mouth. The meat was tender, close to salmon in flavor, but milder. The flavor didn't explode in his mouth, but it had a wildness to it he liked but didn't love. It could use some Montreal Steak Seasoning, he decided. Even so, he pinched his eyes shut, tilted his head back, and chewed, steam escaping his open mouth. He wasn't one to eat seafood very often. The char's flesh cooked up red, and it tasted rich with something, vitamins, oils, the things these people had been surviving on for the last however many years. A thousand? Two thousand?

He nodded, pretended he was in heaven. He certainly wasn't in hell, but heaven was still a lifetime away.

The elder called up the others one by one, and they took their turns pulling fish from the skewers. Stu took his while holding his camera under his arm. Ezra had tried to get Stu on camera a few times, but he refused, whether because he didn't like to be on camera or because he didn't want Ezra messing up his precious equipment, he could never quite figure out.

Doing his best balancing act, Stu chucked the chunk of arctic char in his mouth, his cheeks chuffing in and out as he breathed inward to try and cool the meat on his tongue. Though Ezra knew how revolted he was by eating living things, Stu did a fine job of pretending like he liked the meat. He played along nicely, made that face Ezra sometimes saw when they were in bed together, in the middle of the throes of ecstasy. A tingle shot through Ezra's loins as he watched him.

Next came Jonesy, who grabbed a piece of meat like a caveman, popped it in his mouth and chewed with a gusto too genuine to be fake. "It's good," he proclaimed, nodding his head. Next came Scott, walking up to the spit like a brave pirate getting ready to walk the plank. His hand darted out, he took a chunk, and instead of throwing it in his mouth like the others, he waved it in the air, drawing a smile from the elder.

The elder, bathed in the bluing sunshine of the never-ending night, crinkled his face. The skin around his eyes had taken on the properties of the land around them, rough and wrinkled. Within his brown eyes twinkled something, the mischievousness of age, the freedom that comes when one stands on the precipice of death.

The chief said something in his strange language, and the men began to yell. From the shadows, two men came, holding something red. They carried in their arms violence, a skinless hunk of something that would drive the ASPCA insane. To them, the red body in their arms represented life, a means for survival. To Ezra, it was a seal, a sentient being with a brain. You could teach a seal tricks. Here though, the Winoquin had only taught it to play dead, and once it had, they'd removed its skin and brought it into the community circle in their arms, soaking their own skin with its blood. Without ceremony, they plopped it in the middle of the circle, off to the side of the fire.

Ezra expected them to start carving it, preparing it for the spit, but they didn't. The Winoquin, instead, gathered around the poor creature, its deep black eyes staring at Ezra, the flames of the fire flickering in its onyx orbs. He wanted to cry, but he was on camera, representing a show where tribal traditions were supposed to be venerated. To show distaste at another's traditions would go against the entire purpose of the show.

He cast a glance at Stu. They would cut that moment, excise the doubt on his face, and leave it on the cutting room floor. Stu didn't acknowledge his glance. He had the eyepiece of his camera up to his own eye. He wasn't here. He was behind the camera, a different world where light and framing mattered and nothing else.

With rounded knives crafted of stone, the Winoquin bent down and began slicing at the seal's flesh, not squeamish about reaching out and touching the bloody body. They painted their hands red with the seal's blood, opening it up and spilling out the guts, the older members of the tribe digging through its innards, pulling out savory bits for Ezra to sample—liver, kidneys, slimy things Ezra wanted no part of.

They didn't cook the seal, but ate it raw. Sentient sushi.

When they handed him chunks of the seal, he went into a trance, took the meat from their bloodied hands, and brought it to his lips dutifully. It was gamier than he expected, a wild nutty flavor. He had assumed seal would be fatty, but the blubbery bits, as Maq explained, had been cut off. They would be rendered to make oil to keep their lamps going.

The community circle transformed into a crime scene, and one by one, the members of his crew were fed, fake smiles plastered to their faces as they ate the seal raw. This was the Winoquin way. To deny the visitors their hospitality would be an insult. When Stu stepped up, he kept the camera to his eye, a sure sign he was unhappy with the whole situation. Ezra kept himself from wincing as Stu brought the blood-red meat to his mouth, had to look away when he started chewing.

The old man held up a gnarled and twisted hand, fingers thick from long years of catching fish and living hard off the land. With his ancient hand, he beckoned Ezra forward, the thin line of his wrinkled lips curling up slightly. Ezra stepped forward, Stu curving around to the side, walking backwards, the eye of his camera always focused on Ezra. Some relationships might wilt under that scrutiny, but Ezra thought maybe the scrutiny was the one thing that kept them strong. Ezra was his best on camera, and Stu spent so much of his life seeing that ideal. When Ezra wasn't at his best, Stu could still fall back on those images, the images of Ezra holding the hands of a young fancy dancer, the images of him walking around the parade arm in arm with an elder.

Stu did his backpedaling dance, the camera up to his eye, and Ezra stepped up to the cookfire. The old man took one of those gnarled claws, reached into the skull of the seal. With his hooked finger, he fished out one of the seal's black eyeballs, wrenched it free, and held it out to Ezra, plopping into his open palm. It was cold, and he felt like he was holding a slick grape gone to rot.

Ezra popped the eye in his mouth. He squeezed his eyes shut, tried to do that orgasmic eating thing, but when he chomped down on the rubbery object, cold liquid sprayed across his mouth and his tongue. He chewed without tasting, and never attained that climactic ecstasy he always pretended to reach. Instead, his eyes watered with sorrow as he chewed the eye, broke it apart and swallowed it, suppressing a shiver sure to insult the elder and the Winoquin people.

The children smiled up at him. They had stopped jumping in the air and kicking their feet up. They eyed him with jealousy.

Ezra, still trying to recover from his forced culinary torture,

WE LIKE IT CHERRY

turned to Maq. "Is there any significance to the eye?" Any question to take his mind off the disgust spinning his stomach in queasy circles.

Maq relayed Ezra's question to the elder, then answered him. "The eye is special, big magic. You can see far now."

"Thank you for the honor," Ezra said, bowing at the elder.

Maq relayed his words, and the elder smiled once more, his teeth stained with age, packed tight in his mouth like the rocks on a Winoquin cairn.

From there, dinner was a little more normal, and once the elder took a chunk of seal, everyone went up as needed, digging for their favorite bits, and slicing them off with their stone knives. Stu did not go up again.

Ezra found the meat acceptable, and he ate as much as he could to honor his hosts. For dessert, the Winoquin passed around a bowl of small, yellow-red berries, not dissimilar from raspberries. "Cloudberries," Maq called them. They were tart more than sweet. They were likely the only fruit that grew up here—a special treat to share.

As they lounged around with full bellies, they let the heat and the smoke of the fire wash over them. The women picked up their children when they began to yawn and carried them to the houses hidden among the rocks. The children didn't whine or cry about going to bed. This was the way it was.

It seemed that nowhere here was there an angry face. These people acted as if they didn't know of things like individuality, desire, wants—staples of Ezra's upbringing, even on the reservation with Indigenous people all around him.

When the women and children were gone, half the men departed while the other half turned around, sat with their backs to the fire, all except for the elders and Maq.

"What are they doing?"

"Keeping an eye out for bears," Maq said.

"Bears?" Ezra asked.

"Polar bears. It's midsummer, they're hungry. Normally, they don't travel this far south, but food is scarce up north this summer."

"Can you kill them if they come?" Ezra asked.

"We can, though we don't want to. Better to run and hide. The polar bear is a sacred being; it's big, wise, the barometer of the world."

Ezra was impressed that Maq knew the word barometer, what it meant, and how to use it. Maybe the word was more important here on the edge of the world, sitting next to the cold dark ocean. Pressure drops could mean the difference between being caught out in the open on the frozen tundra and survival.

"What is your elder's name?" Ezra asked, going into full TV host mode.

Maq murmured to the elder, and the elder said something Maq didn't understand, nevertheless repeat.

"What does it mean?"

"Nothing," Maq said. "Our names are family names, names of personality, nicknames. A person in the Winoquin has many names."

"What about your name?"

Maq's name came off easily enough for the first part. "Maquita," he began before u-turning into a mishmash of five or six names all punctuated by syllables and sounds that were strange, almost otherworldly, to Ezra's ears.

Ezra fell silent, and the fire crackled; slow burning grasses, woven thick and packaged into squares, sent up a fragrant smoke. Ezra stared into the chief's eyes, trying to peer back in time and understand how a person could live in this place and not pick themselves up and walk out at some point.

Perhaps the connection between family and land was different up here. In America, if you were Americanized, you understood land as something you owned, not as something that was a part of you. How can you walk away from a part of you? How can you deny a piece of yourself?

Where would a person like the elder go? Nowhere. He would never leave.

"Tell me of the celebration tomorrow."

Maq spoke to the elder, and a stream of slow words issued forth from the man, nonsensical, but carrying a gravity that transcended language.

Maq spoke nonstop, acting as the elder's voice.

"The celebration is a ritual, one carried out seldom in our world. The conditions need to be right. To the north, there is a

WE LIKE IT CHERRY

glacier, it bleeds to the edge of an island, creating unscalable cliffs. At certain times, in the middle of the summer, a way opens, and allows us to reach the top of the glacier. The top of the glacier is a special place, the other world, where our ancestors go when they rest from this one. Most years, the cliffs remain, and this means the ancestors are content. This year though, the way has opened, and our ancestors have things to say. We might never hold this ritual again, for the glacier is shrinking, and the summers grow warmer. This is why I sent Maq to find you."

This was news to Ezra. He'd thought their encounter had been one of fortune, not design.

"Maq says there are ways to preserve things in the snowless world, ways to keep things alive. He says your cameras are one of these ways."

Ezra understood now, felt the importance of this job. They were going to see something no one might ever witness again— and record it. It was all he could have ever dreamed of. Prizes and awards danced in his head as he said, "We are honored you have chosen to allow us to bear witness."

As Ezra pressed for more details about the ritual, he was rebuffed, and eventually, Maq said, "The elder is tired. He will sleep now. So should you. Tomorrow is a long day."

Maq stood and helped the elder across the uneven ground. The elder's strength had ebbed throughout the day, and he seemed like what he was now, a fragile old man, hoping to impart the past to the future, the will of the ancestors to the fertile minds of those who were not yet born. Noble.

Stu let his camera drop and came to sit by Ezra's side. Ezra wanted to entwine his fingers around Stu's, squeeze his hand and let him know how excited he was, but with the other members of the crew still present, the time was not appropriate. They'd been forced to keep their relationship a secret from the network, something he despised, another reason to get out from under the thumb of the Expose Network.

Instead, they all sat watching the fire as it burned low and smoky, chewing through rough bricks of woven grasses at a steady rate.

Jonesy stood up, grabbed another chunk of seal meat. "Mmpphh, so good."

"Save some for breakfast," Scott said.

"Breakfast?"

"Yeah. What were you expecting? Eggs and bacon?" Scott glanced pointedly around the village, taking in the backs of the warriors ringed around them, spears in their hands, eyes squinting against the ever-present daylight. There were no pigs or chickens to be seen.

Jonesy harrumphed and stepped away from the seal carcass. Most of the fish was already gone, their spines now visible all the way up to their eyeless heads, those juicy morsels plucked out by smiling children.

"Come on," Scott said. "We need to get our rest. Getting on top of a glacier doesn't sound like an easy task."

"Sounds cold," Ezra said.

"Layers," reminded Scott as he trudged toward the hut that had been designated as theirs.

"I'm gonna turn in too," Jonesy said, "or else I'm gonna go to town on that fucking seal."

Ezra nodded and waved. "We're not too far behind you."

When they had gone, Ezra reached into his pocket and pulled out a pack of smokes. He had to make them last for a week, had been trying to cut back, but after tonight, after the information the elder had imparted to them, he thought he deserved one.

Stu frowned but said nothing.

Ezra plucked one from the package, put it to his lips, lit it.

After inhaling, he passed it to Stu who took a brief, wimpy drag. Smoking wasn't his thing. Ezra greedily brought it back to his mouth, felt the taste of Stu's lips on the moist butt, knew it was the closest thing to a kiss he was going to have tonight.

From behind him, he heard someone spark something up, turned to see one of the Winoquin smoking on a pipe. The man gave him a small wink, and Ezra smiled at him before the guard faced outward once more. The guards didn't talk, just sat watching and waiting. Ezra imagined, that with nothing to do out here but fish or kick up your legs in some stupid contest, the Winoquin had developed superhuman patience and an appreciation for long silences.

Stu patted him on the thigh as he stood up. Ezra tossed his cigarette butt in the ashes of the fire where the paper ignited, began

WE LIKE IT CHERRY

to burn away to nothing but a puff of toxic smoke. Where Stu had touched his thigh, it burned like the cigarette butt. Together, they walked off to their shared hut.

    Inside, Scott sat reading over his notes by the light of the stone-oil lamp—a qulliq, Maq had called it. Jonesy was already snoring away. Ezra let the hut's seal-skin flap drop, plunging the interior into darkness. The two lovers moved to their separate sleeping bags and zipped themselves in. Ezra found it hard to sleep with the shallow breathing of Stu in his ear and the memory of his hand on his thigh. In his sleeping bag, he finally warmed up so much that he was forced to unzip his bag in the middle of the night. The Winoquin hut did a fine job of trapping heat, he discovered.

    Freed from the fire of his own heat, he finally fell asleep, dreaming of water the color of the sky, deep and cold.

CHAPTER 4
THE ORCAS

"**Bring all your stuff,**" Maq said after they finished dining on the previous night's leftover dinner. The only thing new was an assortment of bird eggs the Winoquin had cracked over a stone warming in the fire. The eggs were not unlike chicken eggs, but with a far richer flavor. Stu skipped the seal meat.

When breakfast was over, Stu gathered his camera, extra batteries, hard drives, and his camera bag filled with a dozen different lenses. With those lenses, Stu could turn even the most boring environment into a living work of art. He wrapped his gear in waterproof bags, as Maq told them they were crossing the water today.

Ezra didn't have much to carry, just his smokes, his microphone, and his jacket which didn't keep him warm enough. Hopefully, they would be moving around a little bit. He might be able to keep warm that way.

"How long are we going to be away from the village?" Ezra had asked.

"Three days."

"Three days," Jonesy had said, clearly not liking the idea of spending three days on top of a glacier. "Do these glaciers ever calve?"

The word *calve* was strange in Ezra's ears, the first time he'd heard it used in such a way.

"Sometimes," Maq said.

"Jee-zus," Jonesy said.

The outsiders all shared a look then. They imagined themselves falling to icy graves from which they couldn't escape.

WE LIKE IT CHERRY

As they finished packing, they emerged from the hut one by one, Ezra hanging back with Stu as Scott and Jonesy disappeared into the never-ending daylight. They shared a kiss, hot and wet, had to tear themselves away from each other.

When they allowed the air between them to grow, Stu asked, "How do you feel about spending your birthday on a glacier?"

"I'd rather spend it on your face."

Stu smacked him in the arm and left the hut, leaving Ezra behind to compose himself. As he waited for the blood to redistribute around his body, he thought of all his birthdays. He hated his birthday, didn't like to be reminded of how much time had passed, how he'd accomplished basically nothing with the gifts given to him. A kind face, a bright mind, the world was not made for these things anymore. All it seemed to want was idiots spouting off about every little thing as if they were experts so more idiots looking for confirmation of their own beliefs could glob onto them. They don't want facts; they don't want journalism. They want someone to say what they would say if anyone cared.

With that sobering thought in his mind, he went flaccid, prepared to step into the cold. It wasn't so much the cold that was the problem, but the wind. As he exited the hut, it slapped him across the face like a 17th Century dandy challenging someone else to a duel. Pistols at dawn, or some such shit.

He trudged onward, digging his hands into his pockets and turtling into his jacket after zipping it all the way up. He pulled a woolen hat down on his head, then felt the side of his jacket to make sure his gloves were still there. Joining up with the others, they walked through the village, across the rocky beach, and clambered onto a traditional boat sewed together from seal skins and bound with a whalebone skeleton—an umiak. The whale bones were sturdy things—thick, big, and white.

The remaining men of the village waited for them in silence, their eyes dark and glinting. The boats were only large enough to carry three people, so Ezra and his crew were forced to sit in different boats, as two Winoquin oarsmen were required to propel the umiaks along.

When the elder appeared and climbed into one of the boats, the Winoquin men pushed off the shore, leaping into the umiaks by lifting their legs straight up into the air, just as the children had done while playing their game. It clicked in Ezra's mind. The children's game wasn't just a pastime, but a practical skill.

They set out over the mirrored water. The channel between the Winoquin's summer home and Tolby Island lay calm, free from the raging waters of the typical coast. Fjord-like, he supposed. Ezra wondered how deep still waters went. Would it look like the vision he'd seen in his dream if he fell out of the boat and lifted his head skyward, all blue and wonderful? As they glided further out into the channel, the water took on a slate color, like an old-school blackboard reflecting the sun above.

The sun shined, giving them a little reprieve from the cold, though the wind still howled through the channel, cutting across Ezra's ears. He pulled his hat lower, tried to find the excitement of this adventure.

He'd had worse birthdays, he supposed. The one where his dad found out he was gay certainly counted chief among them. He wondered what the old man was up to. Was he out somewhere, getting ripped at the local dive bar in Bakersfield? Did he watch Indigenous Insider, call Ezra all those names he'd used back then on his twentieth birthday? Home from college, a bag of laundry in his hand and a smile on his face, his dad hadn't let him in the door. Had instead held up his phone, tapped the screen a few times, and brought up an image of Ezra in the arms of another man, another student from college, where it was supposed to be safe to be who you were. But it wasn't. College was a dream, a place full of lies where people went to discover how unfit they were to live with their families. Promises of jobs, friends, lovers, and a life apart . . . all lies. Sooner or later, you had to go home, had to face the music, which sounded a lot like the word "faggot" mixed in with a bunch of other curse words.

Ezra sighed, glanced over the side of the boat at his own handsome face, and saw his dad in his features. The muscles on the sides of his jaw bulged outward as he gritted his teeth, and it took all his willpower to prevent himself from splashing a hand at the image, from punching down into that cold water and hoping his dad felt it wherever he was.

Well, no way this birthday can be worse than that one.

The paddles of the Winoquin slid through the water, silent and quiet, and they moved across the surface like a raindrop sliding

WE LIKE IT CHERRY

down a window. As they traveled onward, Ezra tried to soak it all in. The world was big, but his mind was small, seemingly incapable of appreciating the sparse grandeur on display. It kept going back to his traumas, his nightmares, his fears. They weighed upon him, so heavy he was surprised the boat didn't sink to the bottom of the ocean. The umiaks curved away from land, and the sight of Home disappeared while Ezra tried to fantasize about a world where he and Stu could come out together. *There's got to be some network that doesn't care if we're in a relationship.*

Back in the day, this wouldn't have been a problem. Back before every company got so concerned about lawsuits, the talent banged each other all the time. Nowadays, even if it was consensual, it was deemed morally wrong, as if one person was taking advantage of the other. No sex between Expose Network employees—it was in the contract.

Maybe, if this festival was as unique as Maq had promised, the world would see him for who he was, and he and Stu could leave the Expose Network behind, head somewhere as a team, their relationship already pre-established. They could be like the gay Chip and Joanna Gaines, only out on adventures together instead of fixing up shitty homes in Texas. Wouldn't that be something? To be out in the open, to be able to breathe without fear rattling in your chest, to be as open and clear as the water around them.

A man could dream.

"Fuck!" Stu screamed.

When Ezra turned his head to look, a cascade of water rained down over Stu. Frightened, Ezra leaned to the side, as if to dive into the water so he could swim to Stu, protect him from whatever was happening.

"What is it?" Scott called.

"A whale!" Maq hollered from the boat in which Stu rode.

"Are you going to kill it?" Jonesy asked.

"We don't kill these whales."

The whale drove up from underneath the water, surfaced, its dorsal fin reflecting the sunshine as if its fin was comprised of a thousand twinkling onyx jewels.

"Why not?" Scott called.

The whale was black and white, its head rounded and large. Off to the right, another whale surfaced, a mirror image of the first orca, maybe a little smaller.

"These whales have long memories. Kill one of these, and the boats are not safe for a long time. It's better to leave them alone."

The orca in the distance launched another plume of water into the air, and then the pair dove and disappeared, leaving Ezra looking over the side to see if they would come up under the boat, but all he saw was his own reflection.

Onward they continued, the world sliding by, two paddle strokes at a time.

For a while, they could see no land, no sign of anything, not even a brief smudge on the horizon. Their pilots were tireless, with their rough hands and muscular arms—not muscular in the way of someone like The Rock, but more like an Olympic swimmer. They rowed without complaint, and if they sweated, the breeze must have whisked it away before Ezra could see it.

Sitting in a boat, with no land in sight, he began to get a sense of just how small he was. His ego, one of his most treasured possessions, suddenly vanished, and the truth of his insignificance, indeed of the insignificance of the entire world, seeped into his mind like a night fog sweeping in off the ocean. It seemed to coalesce out of nowhere, and then he was enveloped by the mental mist.

All . . . so pointless. He didn't understand how a person could maintain their sanity out on the ocean, out on this infinite blue mirror with the sun blazing overhead. Maybe it was because you could be anything out here. Maybe that was why so many people braved the ocean, became captains and first mates and other titles he didn't know the name of. Away from society, away from the world at large, you could be whatever the fuck you wanted to be. There was no one out here to tell you any different.

Though he was scared of plummeting into the water, for a brief moment, he thought to stand up in the boat and declare his love for Stu, let the entire world hear the truth. But he fought back the urge, strained his eyes for sight of land because he knew, sooner or later, he would be getting back to the real world, and there, you could only be what people allowed you to be.

WE LIKE IT CHERRY

He swallowed, wiped something from his running eyes, wished he'd brought a set of goggles like his friend Scott. All Ezra had at his disposal was a set of sunglasses, which he plucked from inside his jacket, cursing as the wind wormed its way inside, wrapped around his chest, and squeezed the heat out of him.

He placed the sunglasses on his face, glad to be rid of the sun's ever-present glare.

A few hours later, the glacier reared up out of the distance, white and shining. A set of thin white clouds like torn cotton drifted across the sky, obscuring the sun occasionally. When the clouds blocked out the light, the glacier turned a cold gray, but when they shuttled off to the east, the shine of the glacier returned. It resembled a massive shelf of smooth ice from a distance, like ice cream pouring off the edge of the world and dripping into the water, the edges of Tolby Island occasionally visible, nature's waffle cone.

As they neared it, the slanting glacier's gigantic form took on the aspect of a massive UFO, the traditional ones like they used to put in science fiction movies from the '50s, round, flat, spinning, easily created with two Frisbees and some hot glue around the edges.

Its grandeur mesmerized him, much more so than the blackboard waters waiting for someone to etch a message upon them. The glacier had a sound as well, an aching, thunderous sound as it cracked and slid, fractions of a millimeter at a time down the slope of Tolby Island. Underneath the noise of its death, a high-pitched squeal could just be heard, as though the glacier itself was bemoaning its demise.

In the distance, a massive mountain jutted into the sky, pointed and sharp, ripping the clouds apart as they slid by.

As they neared the glacier, a chunk of ice half a mile off to the west squealed its last, cracked like thunder, and dropped into the water. Ezra watched as the ice plummeted into the ocean, then waited for the ripple of its death to reach them. It took several minutes, but when it hit, the seal-skin boats bobbed, and Ezra instinctively reached out to the sides, grasped them with his gloved hands. The Winoquin in the umiak with him shifted their weight, treated the ripple as nothing more than a trivial disturbance at best.

When Ezra turned to Stu, he found him standing there with his camera out, crouched low, his hands fiddling with the controls. He looked like George Washington crossing the Delaware, only he was brown, standing in the middle of the boat, and had no particular love for the United States of America.

The glacial cliffs loomed above them, thirty feet tall, their surfaces cracked and fractured, not nearly as smooth as they had looked from a distance. They were like people in that way, perfect and neat until you got to know them, and then they revealed all their flaws.

The icy cliffs offered no purchase, unless one were carrying real-deal, Olympic ice-climbing equipment. But as Ezra glanced around the boat, he spotted nothing of the sort, no pickaxes, no shoes outfitted with crampons. He shivered in his jacket and rubbed his hands against each other.

As they neared the edge of the glacier, he spotted something out of the ordinary, a red circle five feet up the side of one of the cliffs, and his mind began to wonder what they had used to create that cherry red on the ice. *Surely, they had no access to spray-paint. Cloudberry juice?* He couldn't see the Winoquin wasting such a precious commodity on marking the glacier, even if this was supposed to be an important ceremony. In fact, Ezra doubted its significance altogether. How important could it be if they hadn't bothered celebrating it during their lifetimes? Maybe time was different for the Winoquin, a lifetime nothing more than a blink.

You could afford to think like that when you believed in reincarnation, when you believed that, sooner or later, you'd be reborn and able to pick up where you'd left off. All you had to do was traverse the painful rites of youth and puberty, and emerge on the other side as yourself once more.

The seal-skin boat bumped against the glacier, and Ezra looked upward, his head spinning due to the icy heights above, panic in his chest. In his mind, he imagined that small bump of the boat breaking the cliff loose, burying them under tons of ice which had been frozen for thousands of years. Who knew what was locked away in those crystals? Ancient bacteria ready to kill the entire human race? Ancient viruses? Ancient fungi? Killer organisms with

WE LIKE IT CHERRY

immortal lifespans and a penchant for feeding on human flesh? There could be anything in there, and as he stared into the blue-gray depths of the ice, he imagined he saw a face staring back at him, demonic, hungry, lusting for hot blood after a long age of hibernation. Suddenly, Ezra wanted to go back.

But that option was taken from him after the Winoquin oarsmen in the bow of the boat, plunged a whale-bone anchor into the cliff face and began stripping off most of his clothes.

"Hey, hey. What's going on here?" Ezra asked.

The man turned to him with dark eyes and smiled, continued removing his clothes and piling them onto the bow of the boat.

"Whoa, whoa, whoa. What are you doing, man! Put your clothes back on, you're going to fucking freeze to death."

The man stared at the red circle painted on the ice, nodded his head once, and then dove into the slate waters.

The other boats pulled alongside them, a few feet between each one. Ezra called out to Maq, "What are they doing?"

Stu's head swiveled, the mechanical eye of his camera recording everything.

"They go to the afterworld," Maq said, "unarmed, emptyhanded, as our ancestors before."

"You don't expect me—*us*—to swim down there, do you?"

Maq smiled at him, and Ezra wished for Go-Go-Gadget-Arms so he could punch the smile right off his face.

"If you want to see, then you must." Maq smiled once more. "I thought it might be an issue for you, so we stocked up." Maq whistled at the Winoquin oarsmen behind Ezra.

The remaining Winoquin in the boat, shelved his oar, stood up off a box he'd been sitting upon, very modern compared to everything else in the skiff, its edge lined with chrome steel. The Winoquin undid metal latches, and shoved the box in Stu's direction. A wetsuit.

"Hey, man. Can't you just like go up there and drop down a rope or something? Haul me up."

"We would if we could," Maq said, "but the edges of the glacier are unstable. Best to stay away from them."

Fuck, fuck, fuck. Ezra eyed the wetsuit in the box, and then he made his first mistake. Instead of sitting down and using the oars to paddle himself away from the glacier, he reached out for it, setting the wheels in motion. While he unfurled the suit, the Winoquin in the back of the boat began disrobing, that queer smile on his face, his eyes a-twinkle with thoughts of visiting his ancestors in the afterlife.

In Ezra's mind, protest after protest ran through his head, speeches designed to change the mind of his Winoquin hosts. *I can't go in the water. I'll freeze to death. Let us go back to Arctic Bay, and we'll get a helicopter and meet you up top.*

But then that option disappeared, as the other oarsmen plunged into the sea, Ezra's teeth began to chatter just thinking about the death kiss of those waters.

Maq removed his old dirty jacket and the one underneath, revealed his thick, barrel chest, crisscrossed with scars from living at the end of the world. "I will guide you," Maq said. "One by one."

Fuck that.

"What about my equipment?" Stu asked.

"Put it in the box. It's waterproof, yes?" Maq asked.

Stu nodded.

"I'll carry it. No harm will come to it," Maq assured them.

Ezra sat in bemusement as the umiak bobbed against the wailing wall of ice. It seemed each one of his potential arguments was being broken off and plunged into a sea of nothingness. More and more, it seemed like he was going to have to go underwater and swim . . . to where? *Where the fuck am I going to swim?*

"Come on, pussies," Jonesy said as he broke down his equipment, shortening the boom pole and unfastening all the wires. "Looks like we're going for a swim."

More Winoquin jumped into the water, disappearing, leaving the outsiders behind, along with Maq and the elder who sat in his boat, staring up at the glacier's edge, rapture upon his face, his thin, cracked lips smiling for the first time in lord knew how long.

"Fuck," Ezra muttered, over and over, low so no one else could make out what he was doing. *This is fucking stupid. I'm going to freeze to death.* He began to curse Maq as he unzipped his jacket, fought the urge to zip it right back up again and paddle away, back to home, wherever that was. Someone would come looking for him, right?

"Shoulda fucking told me," he mumbled as he peeled his jacket off, followed by his shirt.

"There's bags underneath the wet suits," Maq announced. "Put anything you want to take with you in there, make sure it's good and sealed. The ocean always finds a way."

"I'll find a way," Ezra growled under his breath, "to kick your fucking ass."

As he stripped his clothes off, the heat of anger kept him warm, or warm-ish. He felt as if he'd been tricked, lured into something he never would have agreed to. Go see an ancient ceremony on top of a glacier? Sure, that sounds badass. Go out to a glacier, get naked, and swim to . . . to something? A hole? Through freezing fucking water? Where the fuck were they even going?

In order to slip into the wetsuit, he had to remove all of his clothing but for his underwear. He stood nearly naked, his balls crawling up inside him, his toes rapidly becoming frostbitten, or so he believed. It wasn't the first wetsuit he'd put on, but it was just as annoying as if it were. Now, there was no helpful gay surfer with beautiful blue eyes to help him out.

It was just himself, the boat, and the threat of falling in the ocean as he struggled with the neoprene, skin-tight material. When he glanced at the water, he didn't see its mirrored surface—he saw cold, slate death waiting for him. He tugged and pulled at the suit, the material sticking to his body, his arms straining to push through the sleeves. By the time he had finished, almost wrenching his arms out of socket to zip the suit up, everyone else was ready to go.

He bent down, stuffed his boots, his microphone, his cigarettes, his lighter into the bag—just the necessities. On second thought, he added his wallet and his phone, though neither would do him any good in this godforsaken place. Though they were useless, he couldn't abandon them. In a completely different world, he still refused to leave his own world behind.

As the wind whipped around him, all thoughts of awards fled from his head at the prospect of entering the ocean. *No award is worth this.*

"Well, I'll go first," Scott announced, an adventure-eating grin on his face.

Of, course you will. Goddamn that guy. Everything was a fucking adventure to Scott. Sitting in the desert in a fucking sweat lodge until you were so dehydrated you started having actual visions was the man's definition of a good time. Not Ezra. Fuck no.

Maq dove into the water without warning, and Ezra almost

allowed a decidedly unmanly scream to escape his throat. If it weren't for the old man's eyes, those glittering, know-everything eyes, he would have. Maq, swimming bare-chested and barelegged, carried a rope in his hand, tossed it into Scott's boat. "Tie that around your wrist. I don't want you to get lost."

Oh, Jesus. Get lost? Get lost! Ezra squeezed his eyes shut.

"You alright there, Ezra?" Jonesy called.

"Yeah, I'm fine," he pretended.

"You don't look fine," Jonesy scoffed.

"Leave him alone," Stu said.

Jonesy threw his hands in the air, went back to watching Scott tie up his wrist.

"Bag," said Maq, and Scott lowered his bag down to the waiting Maq still treading water in the bone-chilling sea. Scott stepped up to the side of the boat, plugged his nose with his hand and then jumped in the water. Scott, not known as a particularly manly man, came up screaming.

"Breathe," soothed Maq, then showed him how to do it, short shallow breaths.

Scott imitated him while Ezra tried to keep from shitting his wetsuit.

"Ready?" Maq asked Scott.

He nodded, too cold to form words. And then they were gone, leaving behind the rest of the crew and the elder.

"You wanna go next?" Jonesy asked, his red face grinning to reveal his yellow teeth, his balding head glinting in the sun now that his hat had been stuffed into a bag.

"Stop being a dick," Stu admonished.

"Thought he liked dicks," Jonesy muttered.

And this comment cut through his fear, brought up a whole new cloud of it from deep within Ezra's chest. "What?" he asked.

Jonesy waved a hand at him, studied the water.

Ezra made eye contact with Stu and saw something in his lover's eyes—something he didn't care for—the expectation that he say something, that he stand up for himself. But now was not the time. You don't make waves while standing in a boat.

In silence, they bobbed on the ocean, the glacier grinding its way to extinction above them, so slow it would be imperceptible but for the noise.

WE LIKE IT CHERRY

    The elder stood up and disrobed. The cold was nothing to him, and he stood like Ezra had all those years ago, new to L.A., looking for someone to be a friend, a guide, maybe even a lover, clad only in his too-short swim trunks, a surfboard tucked under his arm, bought with his first week's paycheck as a P.A. fresh out of film school.
    Off down the line of the glacier's face, another thundercrack erupted, and a smaller chunk of ice crashed into the sea.
    Ezra busied himself with his bag, double and triple-checking it to make sure it was sealed tight. He squished all the air out of it, so it wouldn't offer resistance under the water. With the bag as ready as it was ever going to be, he looked longingly at his jacket which wouldn't fit in the bag no matter what he did.
    They stood in silence, and Ezra wondered if their hearts were beating as fast as his was. He had almost drowned once before, along with that very same blue-eyed surfer who had become something much more to him. Though the surfer had been the expert—Ezra had been new and raw when it came to the ocean and waves and tides—Ezra had been the only one to emerge from the water a month after meeting, a month after falling in what was bound to be love. He didn't like the water, didn't want to go underneath, to submerge himself in the same water that had killed the blue-eyed surfer, Gleam. It wasn't his birth name, but the name he had chosen for himself, the one he'd taken after he also had been rejected by his family and moved out to the oceanside to get away from his old closeted life. In the ocean, nothing cared if you were gay. The ocean only cared if you could breathe underwater, only cared if you'd like to feed the fish. Anything else was beyond its capacity.
    As he stared over the side of the boat, the water reflecting the fear in his eyes, he almost screamed when Maq broke the surface, his lips blue, the end of the rope clutched between his teeth like Rambo sneaking up out of the water with his trademark bowie knife in his mouth. Jonesy lowered his boom stick down to Maq, gave him his bag of items as well, and then jumped into the water head first. He came up shivering, the color drained from his pig skin, until he was as pale as the glacial ice at the top of the cliffs, dusted in old, white snow that had begun to freeze and become permanent.

"Ready?" Maq asked.

Jonesy nodded, and they disappeared, leaving Ezra, Stu, and the elder bobbing on the ocean.

"Are you scared?" Stu asked.

"Yes," said Ezra, his voice weak, as if he was on the verge of tears.

"You can do this," Stu said.

And Ezra knew he could. With Stu at his back, he had been able to do whatever the hell he wanted to . . . but did he want to do this? Did he want to dive under this water and emerge in the afterlife, one way or another? "I don't want to," Ezra said.

"You have to."

Ezra shook his head, trying not to see the elder as he stood in his boat, staring at the red circle painted on the glacier.

"If we do this, if we're successful, we can write our own ticket," Stu reasoned.

"I know."

"Then what's the problem?"

Ezra shrugged. Death was the problem. He felt it, but couldn't make himself say it. Couldn't tell Stu about Gleam—he had been perfect, had died perfect, hitting his head underwater when a wave, sneaky in its size, had wiped them both out, sent them diving deep down under the surface, bashing them off coral shelves, and spinning them over and over until they couldn't tell which way was up. Ezra had guessed right, Gleam not so much. That was the thing about the world underneath that mirrored surface. It would play tricks on you, drag you underneath if given the chance, shake you up when you least expected it.

"Ezra?"

"Nothing," Ezra whispered.

"What?"

"Nothing is the matter. I'll go."

He said it because he couldn't say what he really wanted, couldn't admit to Stu, who had backed him through everything, had agreed to be secretive about their relationship, agreed not to post pictures of themselves online unless it was something from the show. Because Stu had agreed to all those things, Ezra felt like he could make himself go out and do this, could make himself take one for the team, so to say. What could death do to you if you

WE LIKE IT CHERRY

feared living in the first place? Better to be dead than to have never truly lived. Or some such trite shit like that. Go big or go home. Although, home was sounding nice right about now.

"I love you," Ezra said, because he had to, had to say it out in the real world, under the sun, in front of the life-sucking ocean, in front of the elder who didn't understand a single word they were saying.

"I love you too," Stu said, and immediately, the water became less dangerous, seemed to be less like the portal to some dark underworld, and more like what it was, just a puddle of water floating on the earth's surface, populated with fish, bacteria, and the occasional plant.

Maq appeared, even bluer than before, his lips quaking now. Stu, sensing Maq's rapidly devolving condition, quickly handed him his gear, perhaps the heaviest box of the bunch. He slid into the water, wrapping the rope around his wrist. After one brief moment of eye contact with Ezra, pure and illuminating, he was gone, and time dilated, like the iris of Stu's camera lens, widening, spreading the world out in cinematic glory, going from thirty frames-per-second to sixty to two-hundred-and-forty in the blink of an eye.

The water slowed. The groaning of the glacier, now resembling the gurgling belly of a famished monster, slowed as well.

The sun overhead sent rays of light at Ezra one beam at a time, and through it all, all he could think was, "I hope he gets through safely. I hope I see him again." His fears, quelled externally because of the presence of Stu and, to a lesser extent, the elder, came back in full force. The water—*it's alive*—hungered below him, while the glacier longed to split open, suck the seal-skin boat into an icy crack and then swallow him whole, freezing him in his agony, digesting him in frozen anguish until the end of time.

Ezra stared up at the blue sky, stopped focusing on the still waters below, on the salty tang of the air. Instead, he locked in on the clouds, waited until he heard the telltale splash of Maq emerging from the water. Above, the clouds scraped across the sky, puffy and warm, warmer than Ezra felt, his feet tingling with the encroaching numbness from exposure to the cold air raining over the edge of the glacier. Invisible, it poured down upon him and settled onto the tops of his feet.

Off to his right, he heard something—the sound of someone clearing their throat. His head snapped to the right, and the elder stood staring at him, the whiskers on his upper lip bristling as he smiled. "We like it cherry," he said, his accent thick, the words sounding alien on the old man's lips.

"What the—" Ezra began, but it was too late.

Like a seal, the elder dove into the water, leaving his whalebone cane behind. Ezra peered over the side of the boat, peered down into the crystal-clear water, followed the blurred outline of the elder as he swam under the boat. Bobbing up and down, Ezra leaned over the other side and caught sight of the elder fading deeper and deeper into the depths, and then he was gone.

We like it cherry.

"What the fuck does that mean?"

He was playing with the words in his head when Maq popped up on the other side of the boat. Their translator and guide tossed the rope up into the boat, and Ezra, sure he would freeze and sink to the bottom of the ocean, began knotting the rope around his wrist. When he finished, he bent down, picked up the bag with his belongings, which had his boots in it, and handed it to Maq. The guide reached up with his blue-brown hand, gripped it in his fingers, and then it was time for the deed—time to dunk himself in the world's coldest water, further north than anyone from his tribe had ever been as far as he knew. But he would see Stu soon. That was something, a thought he held onto, tried to warm himself with, but it couldn't compete with the arctic. When he had steeled himself as much as he could, he stood on the side of the boat, stepped over the side, and plunged into the water.

The sea enveloped him with greedy arms, pressing into his flesh like the stinging tentacles of a jellyfish over his entire body. The muscles in his face contracted, and with the energy of the truly shocked, Ezra bounded upward, trying to fly out of the water and into the relatively warmer air. But he could not fly, despite the faery quality of this place. It offered him no magic powers. But he at least broke the surface.

"Breathe like this," Maq said.

And Ezra wrapped his mind around those words, held onto them like a survivor clinging to the life preserver of a sinking vessel. He bobbed in the cold sea, his breath going in and out, fast, quick breaths, the types of breaths one might make before they decide to finally press the razor blade to the skin and slice upwards, opening up their life and allowing it to dissipate in a bathtub full of warm water.

"Ready?"

Ezra shook his head.

"You're ready," Maq assured, and then he disappeared, slipping under the water like a sea otter, vanishing before Ezra's very eyes. If it wasn't for the tug of rope on the end of Ezra's wrist, he might have bobbed in the ocean for eternity, becoming a frozen corpsicle, a mini-iceberg adrift in the Arctic Ocean. The tug of the rope broke him out of his frozen paralysis, and he dove, holding the breath in his lungs. He opened his eyes, felt the sting of saltwater, but even worse, the cold pressure of the sea against his eyeballs. Confident his eyes would be two chunks of ice in his skull when he emerged, he swam faster, hoping to catch up with Maq and prevent himself from drowning them both.

The sun faded as he dove deeper, the rope on his arm going slack so he knew he was swimming in the right direction. The world darkened, and he was sure it was because his eyeballs were too frozen to work. The wetsuit did a fine job of preventing him from dying completely in the frigid water, but his hands and feet were beyond feeling, and he wondered if he would lose his fingers to frostbite as he tried to surge forward.

Then he saw something new—a turquoise light, rich, almost heavenly, in the distance. It looked as pure as any blue he had ever seen, the type of blue you want to pull into yourself, bury in your heart and purify your soul with; the type of blue you'd see in a certain surfer's eyes as the sun set over the much warmer Pacific Ocean. Between the blue and himself, he spied the shadow of Maq swimming, and that was when his lungs decided they needed air.

As they slid through a crystal tunnel, rough but smooth at the same time, Ezra scraped his arms against the ice, pressing to the sides with his frozen hands. The skin of his palms split, and blood filled the water, ruining all that blueness, darkening it, turning it into an iodine cloud in his eyes.

Maq continued onward, and the slack disappeared in Ezra's arm, the rope going tight. Ezra tried to speed up, tried to press his way through this cerulean shaft, but he was panicking now, didn't swim so much as drag himself through the cave, his frigid hands scraping against the sharp crystals of the glacier. Maq, sensing he was stuck, began tugging on the rope, and Ezra popped through the narrowing orifice of the tunnel, his lungs burning and spots swimming in front of his eyes.

Some people are made for swimming, and some people aren't.

The edges of the tunnel before him began to close in, until they were the circumference of a blue eye.

He knew that eye, opened his mouth to greet it, and the ocean rushed into him, filling his mouth, his lungs, and his nose. The worst part about it was his teeth were sensitive to cold, and he wondered if they would crack and collapse like when you poured cold water over a hot metal container. Would they shrivel up to nothing in his jaw, crawl back into the bone?

He would not find out.

The sea enveloped him with greedy arms.

CHAPTER 5
CATS DON'T LIKE BAGS

STU COULD ONLY record the whole thing—blue-skinned Maq emerging from the tunnel, his frozen feet mounting steps carved into ice that led to the top of the glacier, the sunlight above refracting off ice crystals and lighting the whole scene with an otherworldly quality. Through his lens, Stu recorded it all, the panic on Maq' face, the taut rope, Maq hauling on the rope as fast as he could.

In the back of his head, he was sure he was recording the death of his lover, witnessing the loss of one of the few good things in his life. The camera lens offered him a buffer from this truth, a way to disconnect himself from reality. The image he beheld through the eyepiece wasn't real, couldn't be. There was no way. This was just another scene to record, to document, like all those children fancydancing, spinning in circles, the bells on their regalia jingling to the rhythm of the drums.

There was no way Ezra was dying, no way at all. It wasn't even a possibility. Still, his heart sagged in his chest as blue-skinned Maq hauled on the rope, hand over hand.

Gradually, a being emerged, surely not Ezra, because why would it be Ezra? None of this was real. This was Milli Vanilli. This was a Bigfoot sighting. This man being dragged upward, through the blood-tinted water and over the crystal steps, could not be Ezra. After all, Ezra had never looked like this before. He'd never had skin so pale. He'd never been dragged like this. On top of all that, the Ezra he knew wouldn't suffer these indignities, wouldn't allow someone to do anything to him he didn't want done, and the Ezra he knew, the living Ezra, didn't like to be dragged across ice—didn't

WE LIKE IT CHERRY

even like the cold. He'd spent far too much time in California to ever enjoy the cold, insisted they only film in the summers.

But the most damning piece of evidence that this poor doppelganger wasn't the genuine article was the fact that he wasn't breathing. *His* Ezra breathed, used that breath to smoke his awful cigarettes, to whisper sweet things in his ear when no one else was around, to breathe life into him when they kissed.

Stu stumbled backward up the steps as Maq, and now Scott, pulled fake-Ezra up the stairs. Through the glowing blue shaft, they climbed and climbed until they had emerged on top of the glacier, spilling out onto its old, white powder in a panic. Stu spun, the camera recording everything, the concerned looks on their faces, the seriousness of it all. It was like a bad movie.

"Stu, what the fuck are you doing?" Scott snapped.

But Stu knew what he was doing, he was recording this movie, so he could show it to the real Ezra when he showed up, fully clothed, smoking his cigarettes, that sardonic smile barely held in as he interacted with the natives. Ezra would want to see this, the time when someone who had looked like him had died.

Maq lay fake-Ezra on his side, began pounding on his back, water squelching from his wetsuit with each drumming impact from his club-like hands. The blood from Ezra's palms sank into the snow, dissolving it and leaving behind red slush.

Maq pounded some more, thunderous whacks against fake-Ezra's back, each one sounding like the flat of an oar striking the surface of the ocean. And then, Ezra's mouth opened. He retched and sputtered, and the ocean crawled from his lungs. He sat up, taking half a deep breath before his body revolted, and he spewed up more water.

One of the Winoquin brought a blanket and threw it over Ezra's back. Stu realized it was Ezra, could see it now, as his pinched shut eyes opened for a brief moment, showed him those wonderful brown eyes, the pain hidden in there. Stu loved Ezra's pain, treasured it the way someone treasures the valley a river has carved.

Feeling more in the world now, Stu set his camera down on its side, rushed to Ezra.

One of the Winoquin stood looking down at the viewfinder, his eyes moving up and down, back and forth, as he tried to match the image on the viewfinder with the real world. He watched the skinny man wrap his arms around the drowned man, watched him press his lips to the man's cheek, watched the other two outsiders glance at each other. Then he shrugged, walked on, for the new world was one of lies. This, the ancestors had told him.

"No, that's it," Scott kept saying. "We're going home."

From under a seal-skin banket, inside a hut made of ice, Ezra huddled over a seal-oil lamp, a qulliq, trying to trap the heat. "Fuck that," Ezra said.

Off to his right, Stu sat rubbing Ezra's back with his hand, trying to create some friction, to generate enough heat to get Ezra back to what he should have been.

"You just died, man! And if you didn't, you were damn close. We need to get you to a doctor."

"Bullshit," Ezra said. "We're here. I'm alive. Let's finish it. Let's finish what we came to do."

"Maybe he's right, E." This came from Jonesy, not normally one to show concern for anyone but himself. Jonesy's words gave Ezra pause. "Besides, there's not a single split tail up here. Total sausage fest—although . . . maybe you're into that."

"Fuck you, you piece of shit," shouted Stu, irate at Jonesy's attitude.

"Hey, I'm just fucking around," Jonesy said. "I don't care if you're gay or not. If I didn't care about you, I wouldn't joke."

"That's bullshit," Stu spat.

Ezra placed a hand on Stu, calmed him down, told him it was alright with a touch. "No. We're here. I'm feeling better already. Only thing I regret is that we lost my bag. I'm gonna stay by the fire, but you all should go out there, get some footage. I'll do my bit when I'm a little warmer."

"You're fucking crazy," Scott said.

"You sure?" Stu asked.

WE LIKE IT CHERRY

Ezra nodded, just wanted to be left alone.
Jonesy left, followed by Scott, until it was just Stu and Ezra.
Stu squeezed Ezra tight, but Ezra felt nothing.
"Well, I guess the cat's out of the bag," Stu said.
Ezra nodded. "Cats don't like bags."
Stu leaned in, gave him a peck on his cold cheek.
"I'll be ok," Ezra said.
Stu nodded, placed his forehead against Ezra's, and then rose up, plucking his camera off the ground. Outside, drums thumped. The same as always.

Ezra leaned over the seal-oil lamp, spread his blanket out like someone doing a shitty vampire impression, and tried to trap the heat.

In his mind, the world swirled, like the water underneath the glacier's edge. His memory of dying, or nearly dying, was terrifying. It was so complete, so fleshed out, that he couldn't chase it away.

He'd seen the world before, the place it had been before his grandparents' grandparents had even been born. In the blackness of his dying mind, he had stood on top of the glacier, underneath the winter blackness, the glacier reflecting the green luminescence of the Northern Lights.

The sky-bound wall of luminescence moved and shifted, and within was contained the past, the wisdom of all those who had come before. Their voices reached out to him in a language unfamiliar to him, yet, he understood every word. They guided Ezra, grabbed ahold of him and shook the silliness out of him. All the worries, all the stress of the world, all the concerns about his sexuality, his persona, his career, disappeared. They were inconsequential compared to those lights and the wisdom of the ones who came before. Live, they demanded—really live. Don't just survive. Live.

With that word burned in his mind, the shifting emerald lights had coalesced into one massive cloud, and he'd followed them— across the glacier, his feet cold on the ice, the crystals scraping his soles raw. He walked, passing through a gauntlet of all those who had come before. They smiled at him as if he was one of their own, nodded, patted him on the shoulder with the frozen hands of the dead. They stood in death as they had finished in life, some bent and wrinkled, others, crushed and broken. Here stood a man who had to have lived a century, his eyes milky white, his mouth toothless and sucked inward. Next to him stood a man in the prime of his life, the skin hanging from his neck in ragged flaps, mauled by something, something toothy and clawed. No matter their condition, they smiled at him and led him onward, to the base of a slope, the mountain in the distance, the one he'd seen rising above the glacier sheet.

He climbed, the dead egging him on with their smiles.

And then he'd woken on the ground, his hands shredded, fluid escaping his lungs. Perhaps his vision was the byproduct of an oxygen starved brain, the fancies of one whose body was shutting down all non-essential functions to keep him alive. Or perhaps he had really died, glimpsed the world after this one, at least in this part of the planet.

He shivered. He'd never before been confronted by proof of life after death, and he found it terrifying. The world after this one was cold. The people nothing more than shells standing on a cold glacier as it melted into nothing. What would happen when the glacier was gone, when the sea levels rose and this land was covered with water?

He didn't like to think about it, huddled in upon himself, waiting for the switch to flip, that switch we all have within, the switch that makes the fantastic mundane and fades the edges. The switch that pushes the horrors to the back of your mind, filing them away to examine on a sleepless night when you wonder why you can't sleep, and the nightmares of your past come to visit you one by one, like the ghosts in Dickens' *A Christmas Carol*.

Ezra coughed and sputtered, the remains of salty water escaping his tortured lungs. "God, I need a cigarette." But they were gone, left underneath the glacier along with his wallet and his phone, his passport. He sighed as the Northern Lights retreated to the corner of his mind.

CHAPTER 6
THE DIRGE

JONESY EXITED INTO the night air, felt bad for a moment about razzing Ezra, but then let that shit slip from his mind. No use feeling bad when there was so much good in the world. Maybe not right now, not at this moment. Right now, he was fucking cold, his wetsuit clinging to his body in a way Ezra would probably like, you know, if he wasn't fifty years old with the face of a chronic drunk and the gut to match. But whatever. Some people liked him, regardless of his flaws. You only needed one person to say 'yes.'

With his boom mic clutched in his hand, and his recorder slung over his shoulder by a strap, he stepped onto the flat part of the glacier. From the distance, he had expected it to be smooth, but up close, it was quite rough. Underneath a layer of newish snow, the glacier was ridged and crispy. With each step, his boots sunk through the top layer of snow and met ice as hard as the pavement of his home town of Toledo.

He wore a seal skin around his shoulders, borrowed from the ice house, and stood looking out at the village the Winoquin had managed to build on top of the glacier. He didn't know where all this stuff came from, but it was there. Huts, a dozen of them, big and warm inside despite being made of snow and ice. One smokehouse stood off to the side, made from ancient timbers, their surfaces slick with frozen moisture.

At the Winoquin's Home, the temperature had been in the fifties during the day, not so bad to be honest. He'd been getting sick of the humid summer in Toledo anyway. But on top of The Mothership—as he thought of it—the temperature was closer to the thirties, as if the glacier itself had sucked all the heat out of the air.

In between the huts, a central fire had been built, and the Winoquin sat around it, naked but for skins thrown over their shoulders. The mad bastards sat directly on the surface of the ice. As Jonesy stood scanning their faces, he found Maq sitting there as well. Despite having spent more time in the water than anyone else, he sat naked next to the fire, not frozen to death as he would expect. *Mad bastard.*

Bundles of dried and woven grass lay in a row, stacked like firewood, as tall as a man and thirty feet long. It might seem like a lot of fuel, but if Jonesy had been in charge of the fire, the shit wouldn't have lasted a day.

The Winoquin fire was a pitiful thing. This might be a celebration, but it seemed as if the Winoquin weren't splurging on flame for the occasion.

Scott emerged behind him, and Jonesy shifted to the side. *Here it comes.*

"You shouldn't joke like that," Scott said.

"It's just a joke."

"It's gonna get you fired," Scott said.

"By you?"

Scott shrugged. "If they complain, I'll have to back them up."

"It's just a joke," Jonesy said. He truly didn't understand when the world had become so unfunny, when people had become so sensitive. Shit, give it time, and the world would turn into a bunch of Mr. Spocks running around without a funny bone in their body, talking about how shit wasn't logical. *Fuck, get me off the planet if that ever happens.*

"Joke or not. If you value your career, you'll change with the times," Scott said. Then he pulled that stupid clipboard out, touching a pen to the paper, checking his list like fucking Santa Claus. If Scott was in charge, he'd be stuffing memos about company policy in everyone's stockings, reminding everyone how much everything cost. The guy could suck the life out of anything.

Stu appeared next, his ever-present camera welded to his hand. Jonesy bet Stu and Ezra had all sorts of videos of themselves fucking back at their house. While that wasn't his bag, he couldn't blame them. Jonesy cleared his throat as Stu walked by, "Eh, um, just wanted to say I'm sorry for what I said in there. I'll try and tone it down."

WE LIKE IT CHERRY

Stu's response was classic. He flung his camera up in a semi-circle, propped it on his shoulder. "Can I get that on camera?"

"Get this," said Jonesy, as he extended his middle finger and sneered in Stu's direction, drawing a scowl and a head shake from Scott.

"Come on," Scott said. "Let's get some footage."

Scott was going into pure producer mode, transforming from a somewhat annoying human being and into a total terror with a clipboard.

"Let's get some shots of the edge of the glacier," Scott said.

Jonesy nodded. "You want sound with that?"

"Why not?" Scott decided.

Jonesy took one last look at the Winoquin spread around the fire in a semi-circle, their eyes closed, their heads lifted to the sky as if they listened to something. But there was nothing Jonesy could hear, just that irritating grinding, like someone gnashing their molars back and forth. The fire crackled, the smoke curling upward.

As far as the Winoquin went, it was like Jonesy and the rest of them didn't even exist.

They wandered away without a word from the tribesmen, picking their way across the rippled surface of the glacier, its chill working its way up through the soles of his boots. Jonesy had been a lot of places, but none this cold. He'd passed on an Antarctic documentary about penguins some time ago. At least here they had women, though they all seemed to have been left behind. Plus, he liked working with Stu and Ezra. They were good guys who tended to overlook the more abrasive aspects of his personality.

The ground beneath him was a dull blue-white, the sky above a marbled gray. Though the sun wasn't going to set, it dimmed a bit as it hung in the sky, beaming down upon them. He didn't know how the sun worked up here, had never been good at much in life but standing still and recording other people, but he figured, somewhere in his brain, that the sun above had to be different from the one back home. This one cast no heat at all; it seemed to make things colder, in fact.

Their boots crunched through the surface snow as they tromped to the edge of the glacier. Stu took the lead. Jonesy knew better than to get in the way of one of his shots. Stu didn't swear often, but when you ruined a shot he was going for, well, you were going to hear about it. He remembered the first time it had happened, in Tempe at one of the many powwows they'd covered. He'd been staring off into the distance after some hot bird with an oval face and glittering eyes, and Stu, who'd been recording a procession of children in the Grand Entry, had panned the camera and found Jonesy staring at the woman, ruining his shot.

"Get out of the fucking shot, you thick, pig-skinned fuck."

Jonesy had thought nothing of the abuse, having heard and felt worse in his time. Later that night though, Stu wouldn't let up until Ezra had calmed him down. Most sound technicians would have gotten pissed, snapped back, but Jonesy figured Stu had the right of it. He was the cinematographer after all. Without his images, the sound he recorded would be fucking worthless.

Stu stopped some ten feet from the edge of the glacier.

"Why don't you go out to the edge?' Jonesy asked, breaking his balls a bit.

"Do not go out to the edge," Scott countered, serious and completely oblivious to the fact Jonesy had been joking.

Jonesy smirked. *The man is so predictable.*

With rapidly chilling fingers, Jonesy fiddled with his recorder, gave a thumbs up to indicate he was recording, and then they stood in silence as the freezing wind brushed over them. Below, the nameless water lapped against the side of the glacier. Underneath their feet, the ice, frozen for thousands of years, groaned as its time neared an end in geological time . . . might be another twenty years or so before this glacier was gone completely, but its time was up.

Jonesy wasn't sorry for it, had seen enough of the world to know humans couldn't stop. There was no turning back now. It was one of the reasons he had never had a family; well, that and the fact that he liked variety. The world was doomed. Better to have your fun now.

Behind him, an eerie warbling began around the campfire— throaty, deep voices, all bouncing up and down.

Jonesy spun, the boom hanging over his shoulders like Bo Jackson holding a baseball bat, his wrists hanging over the pole, his hands limp. He aimed the mic at the singers, wondered what the home audience would make of the singing.

To Jonesy, it sounded brutal, like the sounds a seal might make

WE LIKE IT CHERRY

as you clubbed its fucking brains out. Wasn't much rhythm to it, and if there were words, he couldn't make them out.

"Get out of the fucking way," Stu whispered.

Jonesy didn't bother to say sorry, didn't want to fuck up his own sound along with the shot.

Scott scribbled on his clipboard, his head down, while Jonesy attempted to move to the side behind Stu. Didn't matter how he stepped, he crunched the snow underneath his boots, grimacing like a kid trying to sneak into the kitchen for a midnight snack.

Rather than keep inching along and fucking things up, he moved quickly, like ripping a Band-Aid. *Crunch, crunch, crunch.* There was no sneaking up on anyone out here, a thought he found comforting.

"Weird," Stu mumbled, and Jonesy was taken aback. Stu almost never said anything when he was recording.

Scott and Jonesy shared a look.

"What?" Scott finally asked.

"I'm getting some sort of interference."

What the fuck is that?

Stu pulled his head back from the eyepiece, flipped open the display, wondering if maybe the lens was fogging over. The display came to life, clear as could be, but for the cloudy images hovering above and behind the Winoquin. When they had begun singing, he'd zoomed in on them, fucked around with the focus ring as he thought maybe he was out of focus. But no, didn't matter what he did, those blobs hung there in the air.

Then he'd figured maybe the lens was catching some glare, fished around in his bag for a polarizer, threw it on, and discovered this did nothing, just made the haze a little less substantial.

"What is it?" Scott asked, his pen poised and ready to take notes, time-coding everything. The motherfucker would jot down the size and consistency of your bowel movements if you let him.

"There's something there."

Scott came to stand next to Stu, while Jonesy continued standing there like a man who had hung himself, his boom pole hanging over his shoulders.

"See?" Stu asked.

Scott leaned in close, and Stu was struck again by how non-human their producer was. Most people had a scent, a smell you could carry with you and identify, but not Scott. He never smelled, not even at the end of a week. Maybe it was because he didn't have a soul.

"What the fuck is that?" Scott asked.

"I don't know."

Jonesy clomped over, crushing more glacier beneath his shoes. "Lemme see." He leaned in. Now there was a man who had a scent, sour like someone who knew they were going to die soon, so they didn't bother cleaning their body all that well. "Aw, you're just getting ice on the lens."

Stu pointed the lens at Jonesy. "You see any ice?"

"Wait," said Scott, and then he pointed at the display. "It's fixed."

"What?" Stu asked. Then he looked down, saw that the images were gone, those hazy, blobby white things had vanished altogether. All he saw was Jonesy's porcine face, a bead of snot hanging out of his forested nostril. The hair on the back of Stu's neck stood up so hard he thought about asking Jonesy to shave it off. "Wait a second." Stu panned the camera upward, returned it to the singing Winoquin, still busy choking out their dirge. If a grave could sing, this is what it would sound like. "There's something there again," Stu said.

Everyone fell silent, the song of the Winoquin washing over them, a song outsiders were never meant to hear. The glacier groaned in their presence.

Stu couldn't resist. He had to get closer, had to see what this strange anomaly was, though in his heart he knew. In his mind, he refused to believe it. He inched forward, not giving a fuck about the sound. Each step was a battle, a victory over the common sense permeating his brain, which had kept him out of trouble, kept him from experiencing the hate and vitriol the one other gay kid on his reservation had received when he grew up different. Stu knew when to fuck off, when to hide himself, but not today.

Each foot forward was a victory over common sense, which wasn't really a victory at all when you thought about it.

Onward he crept, waiting for the Winoquin to stop and turn in his direction, to tell him to fuck off, go hang out in the igloo with Ezra. But they didn't. As he neared the fire, he thought maybe it

WE LIKE IT CHERRY

was the smoke making those shapes, that some strange peculiarity between the temperature of the glacier and the temperature of the smoke was making it coalesce around the tribesmen. As he neared them, he saw this was not true. The campfire smoke had a different hue to it, darker and more tangible.

He was within ten feet when something happened. Focusing on the white mist, he swore he saw something move within, not like the way a mist might be disturbed by a strong gust of wind, but a sentient glance; a planned, meaningful, twisting of something. That the misty silhouette belonged to something vaguely head-shaped didn't help matters any. He froze in his tracks, clenching his ass cheeks together.

That head, that misty cranial construction, hung there for a while, and he waited for something to appear there. Glowing eyes like in *The Predator*, or maybe the shine of ancient, blood-soaked teeth. The Winoquin song washed over him like a steady fusillade of punches to the solar plexus. He found he couldn't breathe, couldn't do much of anything. In his heart, he wanted to look away, but his body wouldn't listen.

"Do you see it?" Stu choked, his eye glued to the eyepiece.

"See what?" Scott asked, for the first time in his life sounding like he wasn't in control. Any other time, Stu would have celebrated, done a little dance, recorded the moment for posterity, but not today.

"It's like . . . a person is there."

Jonesy scoffed, still keeping his voice low so as not to disturb whatever the hell was going on here.

The translucent head turned, leaned forward, the lower part of its mouth moving as if it was speaking. Then, all around, the shapes entered the Winoquin, sliding into their bodies slowly. The singing of the Winoquin changed then, became more high-pitched, melodic, as if they weren't the ones actually singing.

The shapes all but disappeared as the song reached a fantastic crescendo. Off in the distance, something roared and crashed to the ground, sending vibrations through the glacier, up through Stu's boots and into his body.

"What the fuck was that?" Jonesy asked.

"Some sort of avalanche or something, a bit of the glacier calving away," Scott said.

Stu removed his eye from the eyepiece, glanced around to make sure no bottomless pit had opened up beneath him. As he scanned his surroundings, he noted the darkening cloud cover stretching over the sky. He was trained for that, to spot differences, anything striking that would make a good image. The clouds streamed across the sky like spilled milk in coffee. He turned the camera upward, recoding the phenomenon as the clouds bubbled and roiled over each other like the leading edge of a massive, frothy wave.

From the corner of his eye, he saw Jonesy crouch down like a spider, ready to scurry off at a moment's notice. Scott stood rapt, his eyes trained upward as the gray clouds flooded across the sky. His clipboard came up, his pen scribbling on the paper, even as he trained his eyes on the heavens.

As the clouds pulled over the sky like a gray blanket, the singing stopped abruptly, left nothing but the crunching screams of the glacier.

Stu panned the camera downward, back on the Winoquin. They sat in the cold, their bodies steaming in the night, the heat from the fire dwindling as the grass brick burning in the fire flared briefly and then went dark. A gust scattered ashes across the Winoquin's bare bodies, brown and gnarled, scarred from the day-to-day reality of having to feed yourself, of having to survive.

Silence overtook them, and Stu didn't know what to do. He lowered the camera and turned to Scott for his cue.

Scott looked him in the eye and shrugged as Jonesy reached down and powered off the recorder, pulled his headphones down, and let them rest around his neck like an airplane pillow.

Scott jerked his head back, indicated they should return to the ice house. Stu nodded, and then, like burglars trying to sneak across a floor littered with broken glass, they crunched their way back to the warmth of the ice hut. None of the Winoquin turned and regarded them. None of them waved farewell. They were otherwise occupied.

CHAPTER 7
FEEDING THE FIRE

WHEN THE SINGING BEGAN, Ezra tried not to listen, tried to tune it out and focus on the faint hiss of the qulliq. The oil crawled up a small wick, inching its way to its own doom. Then it met the flame and was consumed completely, devoured by the light. *What a way to go.*

The singing annoyed Ezra. Recovering from his swim, he still couldn't manage to keep warm. In his mind, he knew the dwelling was warm enough. Not like a summer day or anything, but a person could sit in here with their clothes off and only feel a little chill. But that's the problem with being submerged in icy water—it gets into your bones, won't let up, almost as if the ocean itself was crying out for your return. Isn't that what scientists thought? That at some point or other, all life had crawled from the ocean. The ocean resented this fact, like a mother whose child grew up to abandon and ignore her. When people returned to the ocean, mother wanted to lock the door, keep her children from ever going outside again, and even if they escaped, the cold was still there, still working its way through their bones, through their muscles and fat.

The swelling noise of the singing outside broke him from his thoughts. *That shit is ugly and pointless. What are they doing? Trying to imitate a dying sea lion?*

With a pair of metal tongs, like a couple of chopsticks fastened at one end, Ezra slid the wick deeper into the oil to prevent it from smoking so much. The black smoke reeked, smelled of the sea, and he'd had enough of it. He should have talked the company into giving them a satellite phone. If he'd had that, he could have called them up, and had Expose Network send a helicopter his way and come get him.

When Scott had suggested they return home, Ezra had been all for the idea, but he knew the only way to do that was to go back through the water, and it had already killed him one time. Mother waited for him down there, as his real mother probably waited for him at home. But he had his own life, and she was still married to the man who didn't care about his. *You can always go home, they say, but they're wrong.* Some people lost the option, never got it back, and were forced to turn wherever they were into home, surrounding themselves with people who weren't blood but who felt like they were.

The wick settled into the liquid, and he set the tongs down, peering into the flame, trying to figure out a way to go home, a way to get out of this place which didn't involve him swimming through that tunnel.

He looked down at his hands, pale from chill, the palms crisscrossed with shallow cuts, like road rash. He'd stopped bleeding, at least.

Shuddering, Ezra leaned over the flame, let the heat waft up over his chest and his face, and then he felt something strange, as if someone were digging through his hair, the way those old women did back in elementary school as they checked him for lice.

His gaze migrated to the corner of his vision He hadn't heard anyone come in. There was no one else here, but goddammit, something was touching him. When he couldn't stand the sensation any longer, he snapped his head to the side, caught a brief flare of whiteness, thin, like cigarette smoke, quickly before it was gone. He searched the small dwelling, even stood up and wandered away from the seal-oil lamp and its precious heat.

He wandered to the back of the house, to the lowered room in the back. It was warmer back there, as if all the lamp's heat had collected there. A rush of wind entered his ear, violated him, made him shake violently, and then he heard something, as if a voice whispered secrets in his ear. He snapped his head to the side, pawed at his ear with his ruined hand, and slapped at it like one would slap at a feeding mosquito.

The whispering continued—fast, hectic, and—angry. He couldn't make out the words, could understand nothing but the tone. He thought to flee, but he didn't want to step out into the cold. He was already so cold. On more than one occasion he'd thought to place his hands directly in the flame of the lamp, see if that could warm him up, and he pondered it again.

The voice, upon the shift in his train of thought, called to him, seemed to egg him on. He blinked, and his vision grew hazy. Step by step, he returned to the lamp. Sat down with the ease of one who had long been sitting on the ground. The flame flickered, bright and hungry. He fed the flame.

Glorious warmth exploded in his hand, and he lapped it up the way a dog will lap spilled beer. His eyes closed with the joy of it, sending him to darkness where he could savor every sensation. The smell of his own skin blistering and burning, the heat and hiss of the flame. He luxuriated in these sensations. The pain came next, every bit as good as the heat, in some ways better. His mouth began to water, and he found himself growing hungry, his stomach roiling within.

With his eyes still closed, Ezra brought the meat up to his mouth, sunk his teeth in, and began thrashing his head from side to side, anxious to pull a hunk free so he could feed.

"Ezra?" a voice asked. He knew that voice, and for a second, he considered offering his cooked hand to the owner. Surely, he'd want to eat as well. *We're a community, a family, food is for all, not for ourselves.* As he gnawed off a hunk of himself to feed his lover, he put a name to the voice.

"Ezra?"

Stu . . . Stu is a vegetarian. The thought broke him, and when he opened his eyes, he tasted his own blood in his mouth, felt the burn of his hand, and he screamed.

Stu dropped his gear on the ground, and then he was there, wrapping his arms around Ezra, giving him the warmth he had wanted, but which the flame couldn't provide. Ezra's eyes ascended in his skull, starting at the bottom of his sockets, pausing in the middle as something white and vapory escaped his mouth and then vanished into the shadowy upper reaches of the dwelling. His eyes continued their journey, upward and into his brain, where it didn't hurt so damn much.

CHAPTER 8
BONE COLD BY PROXY

SCOTT LUMBERG HAD never had to deal with a situation like this.

In all ways, Scott endeavored to act like a professional. That was how one got ahead in this business. Go in, do your job, be prepared for every eventuality, and when something unexpected happened, have a list of resources at your disposal to deal with it. But this was something no one could be prepared for.

Nowhere in the producer handbook was there a chapter entitled, "The Talent Starts Eating Himself."

This episode is over.

That was the play. That was what you did when something like this happened. A producer's number one job wasn't getting the show done. It was safety. And he had an injured host.

"Gone cannibal," Jonesy said, his thick lips saying the word in a way that would stick with Scott for the rest of his life.

Gone cannibal.

"Is he on some sort of medication?" asked Scott, hoping beyond hope this was just some sort of manic episode, that maybe Ezra had been on something he didn't know about, maybe some anti-depressants or bi-polar medication, something, anything, to offer an explanation for why the fuck Ezra would be biting chunks of flesh out of his own hand.

Stu, tears glimmering in his candlelit eyes, said, "Nothing. You know him. Nothing but cigarettes and booze, and he hasn't had either."

Scott straightened his hair and ran a cold hand across his scalp. *Right. No booze. No cigarettes. That's it.* "Is it withdrawal? Does he need alcohol? An alcoholic can get crazy when—"

WE LIKE IT CHERRY

"Fuck you, Scott. He's not an alcoholic."

"Well, I am," admitted Jonesy as he walked over to his bag, plopped down on his knees, and began rummaging around.

"Alright," Scott said. "This trip is over. We're getting Ezra out. Something's wrong here."

"Agreed," Stu said as he wrapped his arms around Ezra.

Their relationship had been one of the worst-kept set secrets Scott had ever encountered. His heart went out to Stu, but now was not the time for sentimentality. Now was the time for action.

"Right. I'll just go talk to Maq, see if he can get us out of here."

"What if he can't?" Jonesy asked as he wrapped those ugly lips of his around the end of a flask, threw his head back, and slurped at it like a child suckling a teat.

Scott hadn't been prepared for this question. *Jesus, I'm losing it.*

"If he can't, well, we know where the boats are. We'll just . . . we'll just swim."

"Jesus, Scott. Look at him. You think he can swim?" Stu spat, a lover protecting his loved one.

"We can jump," Jonesy said. "Hell, lemme finish this thing, and I'll jump right off the cliff."

"Nobody's jumping," Scott said. "Let me just go talk to Maq."

The others fell silent, and Scott bent down and pushed his way through the seal-skin flap covering the door to the Winoquin abode.

Jesus. Jesus. But no Jesus appeared. He didn't like the cold apparently, didn't come this far north. The only gods who roamed this land came in the form of the ice, the sun, the water. Everything else was powerless before those three.

Scott squinted against the light. He checked his watch, saw it was six in the evening, but the sun hadn't changed all day. For a brief second, he wondered if time had passed at all, but no, when he looked up at the sky, behind the veil of clouds covering the heavens, he saw the ghost of the sun shining through in a different spot than it had been when they first showed up. Scott was clued into nature, fancied himself a bit of an adventurer. He knew the sun, though it acted differently up here, didn't scrape across the sky, hauling night as a cape. It did a slow circle, fading and brightening, no cape in sight, naked as the day it was ejected from the center of the big bang, a glowing ember traveling across space and time.

The Winoquin sat peacefully around their smoldering campfire, the ashes blowing across the glacier, spinning like out-of-control flies, causing Scott to squint. He pressed forward into the wind, crunching, needing to talk to Maq, and to tell everyone it was time to go home. The Winoquin could stay, but they needed to go, needed to get Ezra to safety. Something was wrong with him, that much was clear, and Scott wasn't going to lose anyone on his watch.

Seeing the Winoquin bared to the elements disturbed Scott, made him feel bone-cold by proxy. As he approached, he walked proud, not timid, tried to show strength, the fortitude of his convictions. He scanned their brown faces, their pinched eyes for any sort of sign they were aware of him, but they failed to acknowledge him. For all intents and purposes, it felt as if he stood alone on the glacier, but for the elements gnawing away at his life—the biting wind, the grating glacier, the famished cold, sucking the heat from him like Daniel Day Lewis in that one movie with the milkshake.

He spied Maq sitting in the circle, one of thirty near-naked bodies, his eyes slits. His body was much like the others, crisscrossed with the scars of harsh life in the arctic. For the first time, Scott felt doubt, thought about grabbing his crew, stealing a boat, and leaving without saying a word, but he couldn't do that, couldn't rob from these people who had so little, even though they seemed to like it that way.

He squatted, and his knee went cold in his wetsuit as it pressed against the glacier. There was a humming underneath him. He reached down to put his hand on the glacier as well. The tips of his fingers vibrated, as if somewhere underneath the ice, a great engine thrummed. He pulled his fingertips away as he imagined himself sitting in the hopper of a great blue machine ready to grind him into meat, its gears cogs of thousand-year-old ice crystals.

He cleared his throat, or tried to. The air was so dry, his throat so parched, he produced no sound. Scott tried again, breathing in deep, and let the numbing breeze work its way into his lungs, chilling him from the lungs on out. The resulting throat-clear was unobtrusive, nothing more than a brief grunt, loud enough for Maq

WE LIKE IT CHERRY

to hear, maybe a couple of the Winoquin nearest to him, but from Maq there was no response.

He hated to do it. Loathed having to interrupt their celebration, ritual, whatever the fuck this was, but he needed to talk to their guide. "Maq," he said, his voice barely above a whisper.

Nothing.

"Maq," said Scott, a little louder this time. "I need to talk to you."

Maq's head turned now, and Scott resisted the urge to rub at his eyes. Maq's movements were jaunty and stiff, like a lawn sprinkler, his neck twisting in chunks. Maq's eyes, covered in milky white cataracts, locked onto Scott. He resisted the urge to flee.

"Listen," Scott continued. "Something has happened to Ezra, and we need to go back to the airport."

Maq blinked, then blinked again, as if using his eyes for the first time. He spoke then, words Scott couldn't begin to comprehend.

"Come on, Maq, speak English, man."

Something in those eyes scared Scott, made the cold burn within. If it wasn't for Ezra, he would have given up then and there, turned around, maybe even left on his own. But he had Ezra, Stu, and Jonesy to worry about. He couldn't show up back in L.A. with his crew missing. No one would ever hire him again.

"Maq, it's just that Ezra is hurt. His, umm, mind isn't right. I think he needs to get to a hospital."

Maq's eyes glowed dully, filmy, as if someone had draped a thin layer of egg-white across them. The flesh around those eyes transformed into slits, and Maq, in the language of the Winoquin, began barking at him in his harsh, guttural language. Though Scott didn't understand the words, he felt the sentiment.

All around the circle, the Winoquin opened their eyes, milky dead things, the eyes of a hundred-year-old man, rheumy and pale. Their heads turned on their necks as if their vertebrae were comprised of rusted gears. Their dead man's eyes regarded Scott, made him tremble with fear.

Maq fell silent, turned his head away, as did the others, all except for the elder. He slapped his bare thighs, stood up, his chest heaving. He cocked a finger at Scott, began barking at him as Maq had done, a steady stream of threatening sounds assaulted Scott, and something clicked inside of him. *We have to go. Something is wrong.* As if his finger was a shotgun barrel ready to blast the life out of him, he backed away from the aggressive elder. Trying to seem as nonthreatening as possible, he raised his hands in the air.

He kept his mouth shut, saved his breath for if they had to fight, or run, or jump off the edge of the glacier. He backed across the glacier, praying he wouldn't trip. Something about the barking elder told him not to show weakness. He worried if he fell, they would pounce on him . . . and do what? He didn't know, not in his mind, but in his chest somewhere, something ancient appeared, that instinct that said, "It's time to run, motherfucker. Something is coming to kill you." And though he had no proof of it, he felt this instinct to his core, could think of nothing that would prove it wrong.

As he neared the point where he thought he was close enough to the hut, he turned and looked over his shoulder, lifted the sealskin flap and ducked inside. Behind him, Scott heard the crunch of footsteps.

CHAPTER 9
LIVING CANDLE

EZRA FELT HIMSELF lifted—his body, not his spirit. His spirit was deep down, hidden inside him somewhere. Something was pressing down against it, knocking him out of his mind and into his heart where he felt all his emotions and all of his dreams, but could do nothing about them.

There was something in his body with him—a presence, another mind.

Stu and Jonesy stood on either side of him as his head lolled from side to side, the eyes trying to see something, trying to familiarize themselves with the environment. Seeing nothing they knew, the eyes squeezed shut again, as if hoping this was all a dream.

In the corner of his mind, in the deep dark place he had been shuttled off to, Ezra heard the voice, formed of pure thought.

"It's not good out there," said Scott as he burst into the hut, the sunlight flaring inside before the seal-skin flap fell closed once more.

"What do you mean it's not good out there?" Stu asked.

"Yeah, what the fuck?" added Jonesy, in his typical highbrow manner.

Scott stood up straight, his hair brushing the top of the home. "There's something wrong . . . " said Scott, his voice trailing off, something clicking in his throat as the words caught like barbed hooks in his esophagus.

"Go on, spit it out," said Jonesy, one of Ezra's arms looped over his neck.

Ezra could almost feel the other man's warmth radiating from his body, tried to take control of his own arm, make it do something, but it refused to budge.

"I think . . . I think . . . " Scott shook his head.

"What the hell is it?" asked Stu, his voice rising in pitch.

Ezra knew that tone, recognized it. Stu was terrified.

"I don't think they're going to let us leave."

They fell silent, eyes darting back and forth as they glanced at each other, seeing if someone was going to break and start laughing. They waited for Scott to lift an accusatory finger and say, "Haha, I got you!"

But he didn't. And then—the crunch of boots.

Scott, being nearest to the door, heard and spun around, tripping over a sleeping bag. He landed on the ground with a hard thump.

The presence within Ezra grew agitated as the footsteps neared, like a dog wiggling tail at the door in anticipation of its master appearing. With the last of his strength, Ezra clawed his way from the storage room of his mind, from the deep place he had been banished, using his memories and his desires as footsteps and handholds. Up and up, he climbed, and when the presence realized what he was doing, it was too late. Ezra pressed himself back into the space where he belonged, felt something break inside, and then he was back in the driver's seat, looking out through his own eyes. A whiff of white smoke clouded his eyes and then disappeared.

From outside, someone lifted the flap of seal-skin. In the glare, he could only make out shadows, then he spied something like a waterskin, or the bag of a set of bagpipes. He squinted as blue, glacial light bathed his body. Someone made a motion, and then bright globs of liquid sprayed into the igloo. Much of the liquid hit Ezra full on, coating his body.

He reached up, touched the liquid on his face, found it slick. Then the scent hit him, the gamy smell of seal oil. Panic welled in his chest, and he knew what came next. As the flaming brand appeared in the entrance, he swiped furiously at his face, tried to keep his head from being set on fire. *Not my face. Oh, please, not my face.*

The torch arced into the ice house, spinning, the flames whooshing as they consumed oxygen. The burning lumber bounced off Ezra's chest, igniting the oil. Ezra's mouth went as

WE LIKE IT CHERRY

wide as possible, and a panicked scream escaped his lungs, not because of the pain, but because of the knowledge he was soon to be consumed. He fell on the ground, and the other spots of oil caught ablaze as he rolled on the floor.

The Winoquin outside dropped the seal-skin flap and plunged them into darkness, but for the flames. Ezra was the candle; he was the fire by which they could see. He rolled, and the others came to him, batting at his skin with their hands. Then someone threw a blanket over him, pressed the fur to his skin where it singed against the flames. His face was on fire as well, the flames crawling up his skin to light his hair on fire.

He knew he must be getting better, because he could start putting words together, start understanding the steady stream of swears pouring from Jonesy's mouth, hear the panicked planning of Scott, hear the ragged sobbing of Stu as he cradled Ezra's body.

He had a few seconds when his body was no longer being actively consumed by the flames where he could understand everything, and then the agony hit, the throbbing of angered nerve endings lightninging into his mind. His chest, his face, his scalp, all burned and angry, told him stories he couldn't stop listening to.

"They're gonna come back," Scott said.

"What the fuck are we supposed to do about it?" Jonesy said.

"We have to fight."

"You couldn't fight your way out of a wet paper bag," Jonesy argued. He was agitated, the fear apparent in his trembling voice.

"There's like thirty of them," Stu said.

"The glacier. I'll jump," Scott said. "Just distract them, and I'll go get help."

Stu laughed then, a dark, unhappy sort of mirth. "Oh, great, so we get help in what, two weeks? We'll all be dead by then. What the fuck did you do, Scott?"

"I didn't do a damn thing."

Ezra's only contribution to the conversation came in the form of gasps, clenched fists, gritted teeth.

Stu glanced down at Ezra's face, and for a second, maybe two, Ezra was able to keep his eyes open, soak in his lover's face, memorize the lines there, the shape of his eyes, the color within. Then the pain returned in a nauseating wave, and he fought back the urge to throw up.

"We all go," Stu said. "All or nothing."

"I ain't jumping off no fucking cliff," Jonesy said.

"We are. All of us."

Jonesy began to stalk around the ice house. "This is fucked," he kept mumbling.

"Help me get him up," Stu said.

Jonesy, having no other recourse, picked Ezra off the ground, and the blanket slid from his body, releasing the stench of singed seal fur and human flesh. His wetsuit had been burned through, the neoprene material melting to his skin in blackened puddles, hard as plastic now, fused to his body. Scott leaned forward, peered at it by the dim light of the seal-oil lamp.

"He's gonna need a hospital," Scott said.

Ezra groaned. Help was so far away, and the prospect of pain weighed heavy in his future. "Let's go," Ezra groaned.

"I got you," Stu said.

"I got you." Ezra laughed before another wave of pain drove all thoughts out of his mind.

"We're going. We're fucking going," said Scott, more to convince himself than to convince anyone else. "Once we go, don't stop. If someone trips or stumbles, we're not going to have much time, so just keep going, no matter what, yeah?"

Stu and Jonesy nodded their agreement while Ezra just moaned.

"On three," said Scott, anxious sweat pouring down his face.

His counting was fast, and three was there before anyone could have a second thought. Scott hit the seal-skin flap first, plowed through it and into the blinding daylight. The others followed, Ezra forcing his feet to move as fast as possible, despite the pain in his mind, the pain that told him to lay on the ground, convalesce, allow his body to knit itself back together. The light seared his eyes as Stu, Jonesy, and Ezra stepped into the day.

CHAPTER 10
LEAP OF FAITH

SCOTT BURST THROUGH the door, followed by the others. They found themselves encircled by the Winoquin. They stood impassive, their faces blank and emotionless. If they hadn't just tried to burn them all alive, he would have tried to talk to them, tried to reason his way out of this situation, but when they set someone on fire, you knew that was it, that all semblance of civility had been lost.

He rushed to the south, toward the edge of the glacier, a good fifty yards in the distance. The Winoquin didn't budge as he punched and shoved his way through them. He hoped the others were behind him, able to keep up, and that the Winoquin didn't offer much resistance. Then he heard a struggle, someone yelling, "Go, Scott, go!"

Stu or Jonesy, he couldn't tell. His fear made all his senses untrustworthy. Even the simple act of running was work, as if his brain was so overloaded, so overstimulated, it could barely carry out his orders. The chopped, rough ground of the glacier was a death trap, threatened to break an ankle with every step. Somehow, he pressed onward, not slip on the ground like one of the final girls from the stupid slasher movies of his youth.

The ice crunched, and a great moan shot through the glacier, as if it were yelling, "Get him!"

He never should have come here, never should have fed his adrenaline addiction, his need to see and experience other cultures, because it was the only thing in this world that gave him thrills... seeing new places, having new experiences. Well, this was certainly a new experience. Unfortunately, it might be his last one as well.

Behind him, the sounds of struggling intensified, even as he drew further away from the Winoquin and closer to the glacier's edge. The others weren't going to make it. *I should go back. I should help.* But for the first time in his life, Scott turned down an adventure, decided against it. *They'll be better off if I make it out.*

As he neared the edge of the icy cliff, he readied himself, took a few, quick, short breaths, hoped when he hit the water, the temperature wouldn't send him into immediate shock.

The edge of the glacier neared, and water gleamed like diamonds below. His stomach sunk down to his balls, and he let loose a great scream as he launched himself out as far as he could, knowing gravity would do the rest. His arms pinwheeled as if he could fly, his legs turning ovals in the sky as if he were pedaling an invisible bike. As his body descended, something ripped through his shoulder, pulling a scream of anguish from his lungs . . . well, the one that still worked.

Blood sprayed outward, and he saw it outlined against the slate blue sky before he dropped. His body jerked as it met resistance, and then he was falling in a semi-circle, falling fast and hard, somehow in the direction of the glacier. His body smacked against the ice, and his skull cracked against the cliff face.

And then, with his head buzzing, the smell of his own blood in his nose, he began to fly.

Am I dead?

He shook his head to clear it, sending waves of nausea through his body. The nausea and pain overcame him, and he vomited, bile splashing off his boots before falling into the water twenty feet below. He seemed to have grown another appendage, thinner and whiter than any of his other ones. Then he recognized it, a harpoon like he'd seen in the pictures when he'd researched the Inuit, who were the closest corollaries to the Winoquin. Made of whale bone and painstakingly shaped with sharp stone knives, they had harpooned him like a whale, and were dragging him back up to the glacier's surface.

Blood poured from the harpoon tip, and it seemed with each drop, he grew colder and colder. He reached the lip of the glacier, but no one eased him onto the flat surface. They kept dragging him, pulling him up and up, his back bending backwards as they yanked him back into the world. They dragged him for a few more feet, the

WE LIKE IT CHERRY

backside of the harpoon jittering across the glacier's surface and sending waves of agony through Scott's body.

He thought to stand up, to fight, but he knew there was nothing left in him, in fact, there was quite literally less left in him—less stomach acid and certainly less blood. He rolled over onto his side, staring at the blood spreading around him. Like a snow cone in the summer, he made the ice red, watched as the crystals collapsed in upon themselves as they met his warm blood, the snow melting until the blood had been chilled enough to settle into the ice. *How long until my blood froze?*

He lifted his head, stars swimming in his eyes, and saw blue toes standing in the ice. He lifted his head higher, his eyes sliding up rough, hairless shins, the skin dry and flaky, past knobby knees, riddled with the remnants of scars from leaning on sharp rocks while skinning seals, and other animals, past the shriveled, cold genitals, up the flat abdomen, the belly button that told him these people were human, had been born just like him, past the nipples, small tufts of hair keeping them warm, but not warm enough to keep them from being erect, and onward to the man's face. The Winoquin in front of him didn't smile, didn't acknowledge him in any way really. He squatted down, and another Winoquin came to stand next to him. They placed frigid hands upon Scott's body, began praying over him, gesturing to the sky, thanking whoever they thanked for this bounty... and Scott realized he had seen this before, had witnessed a version of this happening in his studies, just before the tribe... just before the tribe slayed a seal.

"No," he moaned, shaking his head, stars spinning in his eyes, his vision filled with the universe.

The Winoquin stood, their blue toes half buried in ice, and they brought their spears down upon him—hard, forceful, but quick. Scott felt pain, intense and blinding, but only for a moment.

He seemed to have grown another appendage, thinner and whiter than his others.

CHAPTER 11
WE LIKE IT CHERRY

STU SAT WITH his arm around Ezra. Jonesy pouted on the ground, his face a mass of purpling bruises. Long after Stu had given up and seen their escape attempt was going to be hopeless, Jonesy kept going—punching, kicking, biting at the Winoquin to little effect. They didn't seem to feel pain, not like any men Stu had ever seen.

In front of them, Scott's body lay naked and peeled. The Winoquin worked with a grim efficiency, and Stu recorded it all from his seat on the ice.

They'd almost made it. So close. As they exited the igloo, the Winoquin had reacted with sluggish actions. Scott burst through, leaving them behind, but then the Winoquin had closed ranks. Moving as if they were in a zombie movie, they had surrounded Stu, Ezra, and Jonesy. Stu and Jonesy had punched and fought, while Ezra had sunk to the ground, in no shape to fight at all. Stu must have dealt twenty punches to the faces of the Winoquin, and they had reacted with nothing more than mild disinterest. It was like they weren't there, as if their flesh was merely animated, and the people inside had disappeared completely. When the punching didn't work, he'd resorted to kicking, aimed a kick right at one of the stout men's balls with about as much effect as the wind. Then the Winoquin's hands had closed upon them, held them in place, their grips firm and implacable.

Maq spoke then. "Camera," he said, though he didn't sound like himself, spoke as if he was far away, speaking to them across a thousand miles.

Stu tried to shake off his captors, but the hands only gripped him tighter. He was no match for their strength. Neither was

Jonesy, who sat sagging in their arms, his face flushed from the effort, his breath coming in ragged, out-of-shape gasps.

"Camera," Maq repeated. The hands holding him let him go, the Winoquin swarming around him, creating a gauntlet of flesh he would have to break through if he hoped to escape. The gauntlet led straight to the door of the hut. He took one look at Ezra and decided he couldn't leave him behind for whatever the Winoquin had planned.

Over the shoulders of the Winoquin, he watched as they dragged Scott's lifeless body across the glacier, leaving a path of red on the ice. If he left Ezra alone to die, he could never live with himself . . . never. He'd gone inside and gotten his camera, slamming a fully charged battery in the body with a sense of frustration he couldn't hope to explain.

Of course, if he had known what lay in store for them, he might have reconsidered escaping.

Stu closed one eye, placed the other to the eyepiece, recorded the sights of the Winoquin digging into Scott's body, slicing his body open with the simple efficiency they had used to dissect the seal the day before. Down Scott's sternum, they dragged a bone knife. It slid through his skin like a finger through fresh snow. Other tribesmen made excellent cuts along his arms and legs, and then, as if they had done this a thousand times before, they peeled the skin from Scott as one might peel a tucked blanket off a bed, the wet *schlup* of the action echoing in Stu's mind.

They squatted around his peeled body and carved off bits of flesh with their knives, their hands stained with blood. They shoved these tender morsels into their mouth and sat chewing, their eyes vacant, all while Stu filmed.

The elder, his hands as stained and bloody as the rest of theirs, squatted beside Scott's head and peeled away what remained of his eyelid. With a wooden scoop, seemingly designed for the purpose, he jabbed the end behind Scott's eye, leveraging it out as Stu looked on with horror.

"Don't look," Stu told Ezra as he groaned upon the ground.

At this point, Stu's only hope was that the Winoquin wanted to feast on one victim, and then they'd let the rest of them go. He knew it was a far-fetched prospect, but it was all he had at the moment.

WE LIKE IT CHERRY

The elder sliced the optic nerve, pulled the eyeball free, holding it like a treasure. With a stone blade, he sliced along its circumference, put the eyeball to his lips and sucked the jellied innards out, Scott's eyeball shriveling in the process.

The elder tossed the empty eyeball to the side, in a pile of things the Winoquin wouldn't eat, which wasn't much from what Stu recorded.

Bit by bit, they ate the producer, going after the best bits first, and then sawing away gently on the muscles left over. His guts and stomach they piled with the eyeball, but the liver, kidneys, and heart were all consumed.

The hours dragged on, and Stu sat still like a statue as the Winoquin feasted—carving, chewing, all in interminable silence, but for the wet smack as their lips opened to feed some more. The thirty men ate slowly, methodically slicing meat free, moving to the side, and chewing it until their mouths were emptied. Then they'd come back for more, taking turns. It was a communal event.

When Scott's body was nothing but ligaments, bones, and red scraps of stubborn flesh and cartilage, the Winoquin dragged the remains away, leaving behind a crime scene Stu would never be able to get out of his mind. They tossed Scott's clothing on the fire, even his boots. The flames consumed it all, belching out thick black smoke.

The Winoquin herded them then, manhandling Stu and the others into a circle. Winoquin guards stood behind them, their lips and cheeks stained with Scott's blood. One of the Winoquin brought several dried bundles of grass or moss or whatever the hell they burned, and fed the fire. The heat from the flames hurt Stu as his body awoke from the cold.

Behind the clouds, the heat of the sun had vanished, leaving behind an icy hellscape that seemed to suck the life right out of Stu. Or maybe he was in shock. The mountain glared down at them, resembling a giant dog's tooth.

Across from Stu sat the elder and Maq.

Maq translated as the elder spoke.

"We thank your friend for his sacrifice. The glacier thirsts. To die here in the land of the dead is a great honor."

Stu didn't know what to say. He was just the camera guy.

Ezra, his body a disaster of burns and wounds, spoke then, his voice strained as he forced words through his agony and into the air. "We didn't sacrifice ourselves," Ezra said. "No one volunteered for this."

The elder nodded his head, his eyes twinkling.

"A man makes his own path. This land is sacred. This is where we go when we die, to sit atop the glacier, to think, to meditate before it is our time to be reborn. At night, when the sun goes down, you can see us dancing, sharing our knowledge, so the next generation is better. A man makes his own path, but this path is for the Winoquin. All men who come here, who aren't of the blood, must sacrifice."

"It's murder," Ezra said.

The elder's eyes stopped twinkling, his mouth falling open, and his eyebrows raising with confusion.

The elder spoke then, in thickly accented English. "What is murder?"

Maq spoke then, his mouth close to the elder's ear, his hands rising, falling, circling, imparting meaning Winoquin words weren't capable of doing by themselves.

"What are you saying?" Jonesy demanded.

Maq continued his gesticulating.

"Answer me!" Jonesy shouted.

His anger was apparent, but it had no effect on the Winoquin.

Maq finally finished his explanation, and the elder began to speak, his thin lips barely parting as he unleashed a tidal wave of syllables.

When he finished, Maq said, "We don't know this murder. We do not murder. We do not kill in anger as you people down south do. We do not kill for hate. We love all."

"That doesn't make any sense," Ezra groaned.

"We kill to survive."

"You won't die if you let us go," Ezra pleaded.

Stu could only watch, could only hope Ezra could talk some sense into the Winoquin. He had a way with people, a charisma that had carried him through a life of turmoil. But the Winoquin were a different people, a different species altogether as far as Stu could tell. His charisma wouldn't work on them.

"We already die," Maq said. "The glacier shrinks, the seas rise. The polar bears are disappearing. The whales wash up on the

WE LIKE IT CHERRY

shore, too hungry to want to go on living. Our world is going away, because of you people down south. This is our last effort, our last chance to appease the gods. If this does not work, the Winoquin will go the way of the ice. We will dance in the lights, all of us, never to set foot upon the earth again, never to sail the still waters, never to feel the wind. We must try, so we thank you for your sacrifice."

There was no reasoning with these people. This was not a place of logic. This was a place full of superstitions and gods and ways that were foreign to them. Like walking up to the most fervent priest in the world and telling them there was no God; it was a waste of breath, and according to the elder, they only had so much breath left.

"Why don't you just kill us now?" Ezra asked. "Just get it over with."

"What the fuck are you doing?" Jonesy asked.

The elder leaned forward, the grass fire reflecting in his twinkling eyes. His lips parted and he spoke, in English for the second time, repeating the phrase Ezra heard him say before he dove into the water. "We like it cherry."

Something about the phrase bothered him, made his skin crawl. Stu didn't know what it meant, but he didn't have time to ask because at some unseen signal, the Winoquin guards stood up and began dragging them to their hut. Stu let his camera drop from his eye, became part of the world once more. He bent down, lifted the seal-skin flap, and crawled inside the hut. It reeked of burned flesh and desperation, not a pleasant smell.

CHAPTER 12
SALMON IN A COOLER

JONESY FLED INTO the hut, his hands opening and closing as panic welled within him. *We like it cherry*. The phrase stampeded through his mind, conjuring up all sorts of awful meanings. The mind could go anywhere with that phrase, and none of those places were good.

Ezra stumbled in last, fell to the ground and rolled on his back. Stu squatted next to him, and they began doing that lover's thing, where they ask each other if they're alright and all that bullshit.

Jonesy didn't have time for that. He was going to escape, give 'em all a couple of minutes to settle down, to start chanting or singing or eating more Scott balls, and then he'd start. They were in a house made of ice, for Christ's sake. Shouldn't be too hard to punch a hole out the back and then make a break for the edge of the glacier. He'd run low, use the profile of the hut to his advantage. By the time they saw him, he'd be ready to jump. He doubted any of those fuckers could throw a harpoon fifty yards. That's it. That's all it was. Fifty yards to freedom, a quick ice bath, and he was fucking out of here, wouldn't stop paddling until he saw another white face.

He shoulda fucking known better than to come up here. Now he was really in it. *They fucking ate Scott, devoured him down to the nuts.*

"No one's eating me," he mumbled. He sat on the melted remains of his sleeping bag, pulled his bag to him, found his flask, and began sucking on it until he got a drop of the medicine he needed.

Stu and Ezra whispered to each other, soft words wreathed with fear.

WE LIKE IT CHERRY

"Hey, is he alright?" Jonesy asked.

"He's weak," Stu said.

Jonesy went back to sucking on the dry opening of his flask, like a baby with a pacifier in his mouth.

"I'm gonna go," Jonesy said.

"What are you talking about?" Stu asked without looking over his shoulder.

"I'm gonna kick my way out of this house, out the back, make a break for it."

Stu shook his head. "You'll never make it."

"I'll try. You coming with me?"

Ezra sagged in the other non-melted sleeping bag, his eyes finally closed.

"I can't."

"They're going to eat you. Both of you. Don't you think he'd want you to escape?"

"He would," Stu sighed, "because he loves me, and that's why I'll stay."

"That's backwards as fuck," Jonesy said. "Like really fucking backwards. He wants you to live, man. I want you to live."

"I can't leave, not while he's still alive."

Jonesy tossed the flask to the side, rolled Stu's words around in his head. "I can, uhh, end it for you two."

"What do you mean end it?"

"Easy enough," Jonesy said. "Be quicker than what them savages are going to do to him."

Stu turned then, stopped fussing over Ezra. "You want to fucking kill him?"

The outrage and disbelief on Stu's face almost made Jonesy feel bad. "Don't get your panties in a bunch, pal. I was just offering is all." Jonesy turned around, focused on the wall in front of him. "Some people," he muttered as he placed a hand against the ice. It was, as one would expect, cold to the touch.

He pressed his fingers against the wall, tried to just push his way through, but the crystals did not give. The interior surface was glazed smooth, hard as the glacier floor outside. He looked down at his boots. They were durable, suitable for all sorts of stomping around, but the toes were not particularly hard. Still, he was going to need his hands to swim.

Kicking it is.
Jonesy reared back, kicked forward with his boot, connecting with the ice at half-speed. Nothing. Not even a chip or a flake.

Behind him, Stu muttered to a now unconscious Ezra, words Jonesy didn't even bother listening to. None of it mattered now. They were the words of dead men. If they weren't going to flee or fight, they were merely food for the Winoquin. Some people might listen to meat talk, but not Jonesy.

He reared back, the situation grabbing ahold of him as it did from time to time to human beings who were thrown into peril. They reverted, stopped thinking with their brain and reacted like an animal. Jonesy became an animal trapped in a snare, capable of chewing off its own leg to escape. He kicked and kicked, as hard as possible now. There was no other way through the ice, no other tool at his disposal. Time was at a premium. He could have bashed and scraped at the ice with his boom pole, working at the wall like Tim Robbins in Shawshank, but he didn't have that sort of time, didn't know how much time he had really. *A three-day festival. What time is it now?*

Day one . . . that was it. He wasn't going to be around to find out what happened on days two and three, not if he could help it.

The ice chips flew as he kicked, the toe of his boot growing cold from the contact with the ice, from the chips of frozen water gathering around his feet. When the pain in his left foot became too much to bear, the toes within battered and broken, Jonesy switched to his right foot and began the process again.

Sweat poured down his face from the exertion, and the day's efforts took their toll. His face throbbed from the punches of the Winoquin. Slow but powerful, they had subdued Jonesy like he was nothing. He wasn't what you would call strong, but he had a big man's strength, knew how to put leverage behind his strikes in the innate manner of a street brawler, but nothing he had done had stopped them. They were like bricks of ice turned flesh, ungiving, uncaring, and cold as shit. The touch of their rough, frozen hands on his skin had driven him insane. He struggled and bucked like a fish at the end of a line, plucked out of the water and wanting nothing more than to return to a place that made sense. Even now, he swiveled and thrashed, a salmon placed in a cooler, waiting for the inevitable ride home, the stab of a filet knife in his guts, the finger hooking under his jaw, the removal of his entire digestive tract in one fell swoop.

Salmon in a cooler. That's all he was. The thought drove him onward.

Kick.

Kick.

Kick.

He channeled a vision in his head to help him cope with the pain of his toes as he bashed them to pieces against the ice—Jean-Claude Van Damme standing in a jungle, whacking his shin against a bamboo tree, over and over and over, disappearing into a different reality entirely, transporting himself from his mind and down into his shin, becoming pure strength and willpower.

Kick.

Kick.

Kick.

And then his mind pivoted, thought of JCVD dancing in the bar in that same movie, started laughing maniacally.

He fell to his knees, balled his fists up, and put them to his tearful eyes, his shoulders shaking as he sobbed. Then he felt something, ever so slight. A breeze, soft and cold. He opened his bleary eyes, leaned forward in the shadow of the igloo, saw a soft blue light where there was none before.

He leaned forward on all fours—hoping. An icy wind kissed his nose. The tears fell from his eyes and landed among the ice chips. With renewed vigor, he stood and attacked once more, bashing at the ice with his battered toes, sweat pouring from his body now. When his toes could handle the pain no longer, he flipped around, began bashing at the ice with his heels, alternating back and forth.

Stu watched him, clutching Ezra's hand in his own. Jonesy regarded them as nothing but living memories.

Kick.

Kick.

Kick.

When he tired and could barely stand, he turned around and fell upon the ground, probing the walls of his escape route. He could just fit. Somewhere in him, with his escape route now made clear, he reverted to the human he had been, not perfect, no, but not evil either. "You coming?" he gasped.

Stu shook his head, let go of Ezra's hand, and reached over to pick up his camera.

"You should really come," Jonesy said.

Stu shook his head once more, the camera held up to his eye.

"I tried," said Jonesy, and then he turned and began his crawl through the icy hole, pushing and straining to fit his shoulders through the escape route. He went head first so he could see what was ahead of him. His head popped out into the sky-blue gloom, the wind cutting across his face, threatening to freeze his sweat on his body. The temperature had dropped considerably.

The clouds above were patchy, thin, and gray, allowing the dead sun to pour its lackluster light down upon him in alternating rays.

His shoulders caught in the hole, the neoprene of his wetsuit catching on the ice. Panic welled within, and his head twisted left and right, sure that at any moment, the Winoquin would appear and drive a spear through his skull. He'd seen such things before when he recorded sound for a documentary on the cattle industry. He remembered watching the cattle stick their heads in the chute, their black eyes, shining and beautiful. Then someone came along, hit them with a pneumatic punch, took the life out of those eyes in a heartbeat. A pneumatic hiss, and a lightning-fast *k-chunk*; those were the sounds that stuck with him.

He'd never cared for animals all that much, but now, with his head sticking out of the chute, ready for the slaughter, he understood the terror of it, the cruelty. He only hoped the cows hadn't known what to expect, as he did now.

With the image of the cow's life fading from its eyes locked in his mind, Jonesy fought desperately, biting his lips closed, trying not to grunt too much. He pushed and shrugged, a massive child waiting to be born. Then his shoulders were through. He crawled forward, his heart hammering in his chest, the wetsuit scraping against the glacial ice, sounding like church bells ringing in his ears. He pushed himself up, stood on his broken feet, hobbling on broken toes and shattered heels to the edge of the glacier.

He wouldn't look back, couldn't for fear of seeing the Winoquin behind him, their faces impassive, holding those spears in their hands, waiting to harpoon him like a great fat whale. He might be a little overweight and definitely out of shape, but he was no whale, wouldn't allow it. Bent over, he stumbled away from the hut.

WE LIKE IT CHERRY

Ezra's body awoke, but it wasn't Ezra's mind seeing through his eyes. The particular being who inhabited Ezra's corporeal body had cycled through the world a hundred times, maybe more. It had more names than there were Winoquin alive. It had hovered above the glacier for some time now, ever since its last life had ended. It understood the ritual, knew the delicate balance of the world, knew the gods demanded supplication for the mistakes of the beings down below, the strange ones, the destructive ones.

As the pink man went, his boots disappearing through the hole like the tail fins of a seal fleeing the spear through a break in sea ice, the Winoquin of many names and many lives left Ezra's body, and went to find another vessel.

As the Winoquin faded, Ezra came back to his body, filling in the void left in his mind with his own consciousness, relishing the pain his broken body sent his mind, until he had settled in.

"They're coming for him," Ezra said.

Then he was on fire, his nerves flaring in his chest, his hands, his face. His wounds demanded he do something to get better—to heal. But there was nothing to do. Stu squeezed his hand once, and then Ezra heard him crawling away.

Around the campfire, the Winoquin of many names hovered above an ancestor, dipped down into its body. *He is ready,* the spirit whispered, its words blossoming among the Winoquin like spilled whale oil floating on the ocean's glass, spreading in a cloud, floating on the surface of the Winoquin's minds. They stood as one, their spears in their hands.

They broke into a light jog, their cold hearts beating in frozen chests. There are few pleasures better than the hunt.

Stu sensed Ezra awakening, looked down to find him looking after Jonesy.

"Ezra?" he asked, but Ezra didn't respond. Stu reached out a hand to his cheek, tried to turn his head so he would look at him. His face was empty, devoid of emotion, his eyes foggy and dead, as the Winoquin's had been. Instead of screaming and writhing in pain from his wounds, he focused intently on Jonesy as he escaped.

Then he was gone, and Ezra, the real Ezra, not whatever that creature had been a few moments ago, spoke to him, said, "They're coming for him."

Stu and Ezra squeezed hands, and Stu longed to get lost in Ezra's eyes. Instead, he lifted his camera, abandoned Ezra, and crawled to the hole in the wall. Behind his barrier, behind the safety of the eyepiece, he watched what happened next. Jonesy, moving about as fast as a drunk might move after closing time, meandered his way across the glacier's slope. From out of frame, a spear arced through the air, landed just to the right of him. Jonesy's head snapped to the side, and he corrected his course. Because he figured another spear might be coming or because his broken feet wouldn't carry him straight, Stu didn't know.

Another spear rained down next to him, quickly followed by another and another.

Jonesy was almost there. Ten more feet, and he'd be free.

Stu had no hope that even if he reached the edge, Jonesy would be able to escape. Broken feet, freezing water, a body built by Jack in the Box, Jonesy was going nowhere, but Stu admired him for trying, something he couldn't do at the moment.

More spears rained down, one after another. One ripped through Jonesy's calf, and he flopped to the ground. Two more hit him, falling straight down on his back, pinning him there. Jonesy screamed, squealed, his arms doing snow angels in the snow. The spears had him pinned to the ice.

The Winoquin appeared in frame, marching slow and steady. Inexorable. That's the word they'd use on the documentary if his tapes ever found their way back home. *The Winoquin march inexorably toward Jonesy.* One of them squatted low and placed a knee on his back, grabbed him by his sweaty hair, and pulled his head back to expose his tender pink throat. A flick of the wrist, and Jonesy's blood came pouring out. One of the Winoquin bent low with a bowl, collecting the blood. For a good thirty seconds, Jonesy's broken toes hammered on the ice, then they fell still, and Stu pulled back into the hut, retracting like a turtle's head.

WE LIKE IT CHERRY

It was colder inside now. The draft coming in from the side of the hut cooled everything inside.

The hand holding the camera dropped to his side, and he came to sit next to Ezra.

"Jonesy's gone," Stu said.

"Did he escape?"

"Kinda," Stu said.

Ezra nodded, then fell away into the black sleep of nothingness, leaving Stu alone, holding Ezra's hand, wishing for some sort of magic to save them. Wishing for the glacier to break completely, crack off the side of the mountain and go sliding into the ocean. Waiting was the hardest part . . . always.

CHAPTER 13
HELLRAISERED

THE WINOQUIN PULLED them from the hut with cold looks and beckoning hands. For the past hour, one of the Winoquin lay on the ice, his face stuffed inside Jonesy's hole to keep an eye on them. They needn't have bothered; they weren't going anywhere. His dead eyes reflected the small flame of the seal-oil lamp, but other than that, the tribesman made no motion to say anything, no motion to infer he was even alive.

Stu wrapped his hand around his camera, regretting ever becoming a cinematographer. Though, if he had never been a cinematographer, he wouldn't have met Ezra . . . and then maybe neither of them would be here dying. Tough to think about something so perfect in your life and wishing it never existed, because knowing it was going to end like this made it all not worth it. Knowing love but being skinned alive and fed to a tribe of primordial survivalists was a tragedy Stu wouldn't wish on his worst enemy. He should be in Hollywood, recording gay porn, or on the set of *Transformers 12*, nodding his head at Michael Bay and pretending the man was a genius. Any of those fates trumped this current one—recording the Winoquin as they feasted upon his friends.

With Ezra hanging off his left shoulder, Stu stumbled out through the seal-skin flap and stepped into the glacial wind pouring down the slopes of the mountain to the north. The sun above, so welcome earlier, had become the bane of Stu's existence. Ever-glaring, never bright enough or warm enough, it still supplied enough light for Stu to witness every abhorrent moment—every foul slurp, every nasty bunching of the jaw and drip of blood from the lips as the Winoquin fed. This business would be better done in the dark, where shadows provided some air of mystery, where the darkness would turn the blood black, instead of that vivid heart-pumping red, the mere sight of it filling him with panic.

The Winoquin stood around Stu, forming their gauntlet of flesh—as if he were going to try to escape. But he'd hitched himself to Ezra, had declared his love and loyalty to him, pledged his life, and what kind of man would he be if he went back on that? Not a man at all, really.

At the end of the flesh gauntlet, Jonesy lay on the ground, his body already skinned.

Ezra's head lolled on his neck, his eyes opening for a moment before he buried his face in Stu's shoulder, with the word "Fuck," escaping his lips like a prayer as he took in the horrid sight of Jonesy's *Hellraiser*ed body.

On the other side of the body knelt the elder, his face still painted with the bloody handprints he'd left as he fed himself.

The elder's arms, thin and ancient, raised in the air, and he gestured, hands held out flat in the universal signal to sit.

"He wants us to sit," Stu said to Ezra.

Ezra sobbed a bit, and Stu wondered what was happening in his head, where he was going, and if he would disappear sooner or later. Stu, still recording, lowered himself to the snow, dragging Ezra along with him, his hands tight around his bicep, his other arm holding the camera up to his eye.

The elder pinched his fingers together, held them up to his mouth and made a chewing gesture. Then he pointed at Jonesy's body.

It wasn't that Stu didn't understand what he was implying, it's that the thought that such a thing could be possible had never crossed his mind, so as the elder continued indicating for Stu and Ezra to feast on their former sound operator, Stu couldn't quite put the idea together.

Maq spoke then, as himself, not the possessed demon he had been a few hours ago. "You must eat," Maq said.

When Stu turned the camera on him, he saw no more of those milky outlines, no more spirits inhabiting the living.

"I can't eat my friend," Stu said.

"I won't," Ezra added.

As Stu's knees froze on the glacial ice, Maq nodded his head, spoke to the elder, presumably relaying their answers.

The elder nodded his head, his eyes twinkling for the first time since the Winoquin had started chanting. Maq translated once more.

"Survival is the truth. Survival is the goal. These men died so we might survive."

"We could eat fish, seal, whales," Stu countered as Ezra gibbered on his arm.

"This survival is different. This is survival of the soul. Our tribe grows stale, grows flat. We were never meant to be, never meant to make it this far, but we found our way, fought and kicked and screamed, and now the world punishes us, takes away the glaciers, takes away the polar bears, all because we decided to live longer than we should have. When the pale men first came, we were on the verge of extinction, of being no more. But then, on this glacier, in this very same place, we renewed ourselves, under the eyes of our ancestors, those who long to be born once more, and the cycle began again. This is the ceremony—renewal, rebirth, extension. This is the last one, by the time it will be needed again, the world will have changed once more, our glacier will be gone, our spirits with them, and one by one we will all disappear, cease to be. But while there are spirits, while the land of the dead still exists, while they call to us in the long nights, we will honor their wishes."

Stu shook his head, though his camera recorded all.

"The ceremony requires you to eat, feast, open yourself to the renewal," Maq translated.

Ezra leaned forward looking at the skinned corpse of Jonesy. His hand snaked out.

"What are you doing?" Stu asked.

"It's the ceremony," Ezra said.

Stu shook his head. "I can't."

"Do it," Ezra said as he plucked at the tender fibers of Jonesy.

"I can't," Stu said, his voice catching in his throat.

"You can."

Ezra's attempts at pulling a tender morsel from Jonesy's body failed. "Do you have something I can cut with?" Ezra asked.

Maq bent down, handed Ezra an onyx cutting tool, its end semi-circular and razor-sharp. He leaned forward, pressing the blade through Jonesy's muscle fibers, slicing a chunk from his thigh as the blood pooled underneath his body. Ezra's fingers turned red, as did the handle of the cutting tool. When he had a chunk of meat, he turned and placed it in Stu's hand. "Eat," he begged.

"I'm . . . I'm a vegetarian."

"If anyone was ever a vegetable, it was Jonesy," Ezra countered.

The elder moved, squat-walking to Jonesy's head. From the ground, he pulled his eye-plucking scoop, jabbed it behind Jonesy's peeper, leveraged it out, and sliced the optic nerve. With similarly bloody hands, the elder held Jonesy's eyeball out to Ezra.

He traced a line along the eyeball with his knife, gestured and mimicked how Ezra should enjoy this rare delicacy. Stu's stomach churned as he watched Ezra reach out and accept the gift.

"What are you doing?" Stu hissed.

"We're finishing the show."

"What? Why?"

"Because, if we don't get out of this, I want people to see how heroic and brave we were, not how scared we were. If we do get out of this, well, even better." With that, Ezra put Jonesy's eyeball up to his lips, squeezed on it until the slit opened in a vaguely sapphic shape, and tipped his head back, sucking the juices from the rubbery orb.

Ezra dry-heaved for a second, and Stu zoomed in on his face. His lover turned to him, seemed to sense whenever Stu focused the camera on him. "Not good, but not bad either," Ezra said, as Stu fought his own bile.

The time counter in Stu's display clicked over to midnight and Stu said, "This is the worst birthday party anyone has ever had." Ezra elbowed him in the ribs good-naturedly.

"It is your birthday?" Maq asked, his curiosity piqued.

Ezra nodded, and Stu marveled at how he was holding it together, how he was keeping himself upright despite his gnawed hand and the burns covering his body. For the second time since seeing the white shapes, he wondered if maybe this place was truly magical.

Maq squatted down to the elder's side and spoke with his head turning left and right as he addressed the other Winoquin. Finally, Maq switched back to English.

"This is a special day," Maq said. "How lucky for you to be in the land of the dead on the day of your birth."

"Yeah, feels lucky," Ezra said.

Maq nodded, missing the sarcasm in Ezra's voice. Stu continued recording as the other Winoquin crowded in, smiles on their faces for the first time in a long time.

"What are your birthdays like?" Ezra asked as he held a chunk of meat up to his mouth, cold and red.

Maq spoke easily and freely, unconcerned about having killed two of Stu and Ezra's friends. Meanwhile, the Winoquin, their knives in their hands, leaned forward on hands and knees, each one slicing one-handed at meat and plucking chunks free with the practiced ease of the best butchers back in the real world. Any one of these men could be rich among polite society if they opened a butcher shop.

"Birthdays are very special to us," Maq said. "On this day, all the spirits visit you, come to you to impart their wisdom into your body. A person on their birthday must be obeyed, must be revered because you never know which ancestor is visiting them at that moment. The ancestors, for a while, they share the body with the living, and so, whatever they ask for, we gift. This is how birthdays work among the Winoquin."

"So, right now, you believe the ancestors are within me."

Maq smiled, his white teeth reflecting the blue sun above. "You are not family. They will not come visit you." He repeated what Ezra said to the others, and they laughed, the men nearest Ezra slapping him on the back good-naturedly.

"But they have visited me," Ezra said.

At this, the smile fell from Maq's face. The elder, sensing the shift in Maq's disposition, tapped him on the knee, uttered a question. Maq leaned over, spoke into the elder's ear.

Ezra handed Stu another chunk of Jonesy, begged him to eat. "Come on," Ezra said. You'll need the energy."

"I just can't," Stu said. "I'm not like you. I can't just do that."

"Do it for me."

Before Stu could rebuff Ezra again, he reached out, pressed a chunk of cold meat onto his fingertips. Stu closed his eyes. His first instinct was to throw the meat upon the ground but he knew this might be a horrible insult to the tribesmen, to flat out waste food

WE LIKE IT CHERRY

in front of the Winoquin, a people who valued every inch of a carcass. Even after all they had done to them, Stu couldn't do that, so he sat with the meat cooling on his fingertips, the temperature of the blood-soaked flesh dropping and dropping until he thought the meat—Jonesy—was going to freeze to his fingertips. In the end, the thought of Jonesy chunks freezing to his fingers drove him to bring his hand up to his mouth. In the past twenty years of Stu Nofire's thirty-year-life, he had been a vegetarian, only sometimes eating fish. Fish were unfeeling animals, he'd always reasoned. Now, a chunk of a living, breathing, thinking man sat on his tongue, warming in his mouth.

Bile flooded the back of his throat, and like a child downing a Brussel sprout, he chewed the meat as fast as he could, chomping down on the tough fibers as his molars mushed coppery blood from the flesh. He chewed faster and faster, his eyes pinched closed in concentration. When it was ready, when it had been masticated to the point of being swallowable, he tried to do it, tried to send Jonesy into his guts . . . but then it was if he had forgotten how to swallow altogether. The meat sat in the back of his throat, and panic welled inside him as his mouth filled with saliva, an autonomic response to having salty meat in his mouth. If he didn't figure out the trick to swallowing, he would suffocate on his own spit and Jonesy's blood. He squeezed his eyes shut, dipped his chin down at his chest, squeezed his eyes so tight his eyeballs hurt, and then it went plunking into his stomach. He could breathe, but the lingering taste of Jonesy's blood made him want to puke even more. Mustering all his will, he resisted the urge to spit upon the ground.

When he opened his eyes, Ezra nodded at him, even as he plunked another chunk of their soundman into his own mouth.

Over the course of the feast, Stu recorded hours of footage, the Winoquin escorting him to the hut every time he needed to grab another memory card or swap out batteries. When Jonesy—may he rest in peace—was nothing more than a red *Castlevania* skeleton covered in blood and wiry ligaments and tendons, the Winoquin escorted the two remaining outsiders back to their hut, the noxious smell of Jonesy's clothing burning on the campfire hanging on the air.

At the back of the hut, one of the Winoquin was laying there in the hole Jonesy had made, his eyes closed, snoring on top of a seal skin. They wouldn't be able to escape that way.

Maq bid them goodnight, told Ezra and Stu to get some sleep. "Tomorrow is going to be long," he said.

"Longer than today?"

"Yes."

With that, Maq departed, and Stu set his camera down, busied himself with heaping their remaining blankets into a great pile so he and Ezra could nest together. When he was done, he lay down, pulling the charred seal-skin blankets over the top of them.

CHAPTER 14
NEW FRUIT

EZRA RESISTED THE urge to awaken. Though his dreams were nightmarish, he knew pain awaited if he woke, knew his singing nerves would drive him mad, so he held onto the void, reveled in it, even as the world darkened.

Though he wanted to dream about home, about all the places he'd been, all the fairgrounds with the stink of fry bread on the air, the smell of dust, of growing grass being trampled underfoot, these were not the dreams that came to him.

Instead, he was born again on an island of blue, on the shifting, complaining glacier. He wandered along the ice, sure-footed, warm within his clothing, layer after layer keeping him nice and toasty. His hands clutched a spear, carved from whale bone. It was then he understood he wasn't himself.

He was a passenger in someone else's body, going along for the ride. Something important was happening, a vision from the dead he hoped he could understand, a vision that could maybe save Stu's life, maybe even his own, though he knew that was too much to ask for.

To his side strode other Winoquin, brothers and uncles and fathers, sometimes all in one. They tracked multiple sets of footprints across the ice, enjoying the hunt. The hunt made you warm, and at the end, if you did your job well, and the spirits lauded you for your efforts, there would be food.

Onward they trudged, implacable, using the butts of their spears to tap on the ice, lest a crevasse open up underneath them. Many relatives had perished to the hungry glacier, but over the centuries they had learned its ways. At night, watching the green lights glow, their relatives spoke of the ways they'd died, not to lament, but to warn, to keep the tribe going, to keep them strong and healthy. All were loved, the dead and the living. There was no room for pouting, no room for thinking about fate or the way the world treated you. To be alive was the goal. To keep going. To feed, so you could spend time laughing and enjoying the family, the tribe. This was all that mattered.

Should death come for him, he would fight, because fighting was life. But should he fail, he would not cry or pout, because he knew he would be reborn again after spending time in the land of the dead, among the ancients, the yet unborn, patiently awaiting their return.

The footsteps they tracked traveled up the side of the mountain, frantic, switching back and forth. The Winoquin strode straight and easy, gaining ground because they were not panicked or concerned. Their prey was a different story. Many times, they found evidence of their quarry slipping and stumbling on the ice, the pristine glacier's surface disturbed by handprints and body-sized indentations. The footsteps dragged. Their prey tired.

Their quarry would need to rest soon, had spent all their energy trying to escape, but the Winoquin moved like the glacier itself, slow and steady, undeniable.

The outsiders appeared as dots first. They had run a long way, their legs taking them far away from the shore as the Winoquin had swarmed over them. It was the time, the stairway to the land of the dead had opened, and these men had appeared. It was the sign. It was time for the ritual, the one that kept their tribe going, even when the world seemed to want no more of them.

The strangers shambled in strange clothes. Encounters with the outsiders had become more and more frequent. At first, they were like the others, the tribe who lived off to the west with their sleds and their dogs and their boats . . . they just wanted to trade. But then they had become more violent, more demanding. A bad wind had swept through the village, and the strange men took what they wanted—women, children, ancient artifacts of power that kept the tribe safe. Now, with the bad wind filling the people, making their bodies swell with strange lumps, making them cough up blood and go to the land of the dead sooner than necessary, the Winoquin eschewed all outsiders. Their belongings remained

WE LIKE IT CHERRY

packed, ready to move, and they wandered the ice sheets in the winter, surviving by moving from spot to spot, lest the outsiders find them again.

But it was summer and the outsiders grew bolder, pressed in on their lands, wanted to find the people—some to trade, others to plunder. It was the time! The passage to the land of the dead had opened once more, and they knew the world was about to be righted. The passage only opened in times of great need, and now was one such time.

Ahead, the black dots became men, their white skin flushed pink, clouds of steam pouring from their bodies. They were losing water and energy. But the blood would be evenly distributed for their efforts. The pinker the skin the better, this the ancestors howled to him from the other world. The men didn't want to eat their human quarry, but the spirits, the dead, needed an infusion of life to help the tribe.

They'd brought the men here among the spirits, a sacrifice for their starved ancestors. Their forefathers and foremothers inhabited their bodies now, a warm thing, comforting, and they drove the meat onward, insuring it was properly seasoned.

As they closed in on the stumbling quarry, their arms raised in the air, stiff from not existing, from not being a hundred percent in control of the bodies they inhabited. The spears flew, one by one, a pointed rain. Their victims screamed out, their red blood, like the Winoquin's own, spilling out upon the thirsty glacier where the ice and snow slurped it up.

The spirit bodies gathered around the victims. One of the outsiders, blonde-haired, blue eyes as if the colorless glacier itself gave birth to him, reached into a pocket, brought out a handful of strange, rounded objects. A stem, wooden and split, connected the most beautiful fruits. The red was so bright, the skin so shiny, that the Winoquin stayed their killing blows, reached out for the offering.

It was better than blood; that red purer. Round and round, they passed the fruits, marveling at their perfect skin, the red gleaming underneath the ever-present sun of summer. The pink man, spears through his leg and shoulder, indicated they should eat it, and one by one, they took the smallest nibbles, like fish kissing the surface of the ocean. Smiles broke across their face, a rarity for the dead inhabiting the living.

"It's a cherry," the man said.

The Winoquin glanced down at him, confused. This man's words were like the babbling of a baby to them.

With a pale finger, the man pointed at the object held in one man's hand, said, "Cherry," once more.

"Cherry," the Winoquin said. And then they nodded, told the man he had made a good deal.

His friends offered no such gifts, so they delivered the killing blows, and then dragged their bodies back to the base of the glacier, where they feasted all night, eating the flesh, but still dreaming of cherries. The man who offered them his gift died that night from blood loss, or perhaps from the shock of seeing men eating other men. They shoved him into a crevasse and let him become a part of the glacier. Later, after the ceremony, after the dead, willful spirits returned to the skies, the living Winoquin searched the outsiders' boats for more of the fruits, but they found nothing, and tore the boat apart for other uses. That spring, ten baby Winoquin were born, and no outsiders visited them.

They like it cherry, their flesh and their fruit.

Ezra sat up, his nerves screaming at him, so loud, his body couldn't emulate them.

The light through Jonesy's hole was the same, as was the face. Trapped in the ice hut, he thought about what he had dreamed, wondered if any of it was true, or if he was having visions. Even if it was true, he had no idea how to use the information against the Winoquin. *Not everything has an answer. Not everything is a test. Sometimes, death is just the way it is.*

He waited a long time for Stu to awaken. It was better asleep, away from the cold breeze drifting through the igloo, but he had thinking to do. As he waited for Stu, Ezra's good hand opened and clenched as he tried to come up with a way to save their lives.

CHAPTER 15
BIRTHDAY WISH

ON THE SECOND DAY, the Winoquin came inside and woke Stu up.

"Camera," Maq said.

Outside, they sat around the fire amid the blood-stained snow and the washed-out world. The colors weren't right up here, faded and dim, a terrible place to be, Stu decided.

With his camera in hand, fully charged, a new memory card inserted inside, he waited for the inevitable, the moment when the Winoquin would kill one of them and feast. He had a feeling Ezra was next. Stu didn't know if he could record his lover being eaten.

"Maq," he pleaded.

Maq arched an eyebrow at him from the circle, but said no more.

"Maq. I can teach you how to run the camera."

Maq shook his head. "These things, the Southerner things are not for me. They are—" Maq said some word Stu didn't understand, but he got the meaning as Maq slashed a hand across his throat.

"Forbidden," Stu guessed.

Stu groped for the words, tried to find something that would break through culture and inevitability. Words were magic, they could do anything for you, maybe even keep you from having to record a loved one's body being consumed.

"I love him," Stu said.

Ezra's head turned toward him, but before he could say anything, Stu continued.

"I can't record him . . . being sacrificed." Even now, after everything he'd seen, he couldn't say the word "eaten" out loud. That would make it too real.

"You are lovers?" Maq asked.

The elder asked something in a questioning tone, his eyebrows raised.

Maq spoke to him, gesturing at Ezra and Stu.

The elder nodded his head as he looked at the pair. Everything went still, but for the grass burning on the fire, the small smudge of smoke curling upwards into the clear sky, which somehow looked colder than the glacier itself. The elder pondered for a moment, and then he spoke, Maq translating for him.

"You are like the orca. Mate for life. To kill an orca, but leave the mate alive is bad luck, very bad. The orca left alive always returns, angry, destroys boats, destroys the Winoquin. We had thought to let you leave after the ceremony, show the footage to the others, so our traditions might live on."

"What?" Stu asked, news they were planning on letting him live, hitting him in the chest like a sledgehammer.

"But it is too late. Kill none, or both, or one? Kill none and the ritual is incomplete. We die, all the Winoquin, but you live. Kill both, and then there's no one to record our traditions, to carry them to the people of the south and let them know they are killing us. We die anyway. Kill one and face the curse of the Orca. This is the decision we have to make."

The elder leaned over the smoke, grabbed a handful of it and washed it over his head, chewing on his lower lip. The Winoquin leaned forward on their knees, awaiting the man's proclamation.

"Go then, back to the hut. We must discuss."

The Winoquin led Stu and Ezra back to the igloo, and for the first time, he saw doubt in their eyes. They didn't smile or laugh, but something in their twinkling eyes said things had changed.

Inside the hut, Ezra laid into him. "You fucking idiot. They were going to let you go."

"I was trying to save you."

"I didn't ask you to save me," Ezra screamed. "And now you're gonna die too."

"Maybe they won't kill us," Stu said.

Ezra reached out his one good hand, gripped Stu's, and they sat next to each other, awaiting their fate, knowing they had messed up.

Outside, the Winoquin began to chant, calling on the spirits of

WE LIKE IT CHERRY

the dead. Their song rose up, flat and formless, like the glacier itself, their gravelly, seldom-used voices finding a pitch the frightened couple had yet to hear.

Ezra and Stu clung to each other, reveling in each other's warmth, resigning themselves to the end. It's comforting to know you're going to die and there's nothing you can do about it, like giving in to sleep and letting your parents carry you from the back of the car to your bed at the end of a long road trip. It's lovely to know your responsibilities are over, your duties finished. With nothing else to do, they savored each other's breath, the warmth, the sound of each other's beating hearts.

Outside the song swelled, went on and on for hours. Inside the hut, Ezra and Stu sang a different song, wordless, but no less powerful.

When the song ended, they sat up, the breeze from Jonesy's hole stealing the heat they managed to conserve. "They're coming," Stu said.

"I'm not afraid," Ezra said.

"Fuck you. I'm scared out of my mind."

"Don't be."

Stu didn't know how Ezra could be so calm, but his tranquility stole over him, whether he intended it to or not. When Maq appeared behind the seal-skin flap, they were ready, came without being bidden, the camera clutched in Stu's right hand, Ezra clinging to his right shoulder. Whatever remained of their closeness was whipped away by the cutting wind. If they were looking for answers on Maq's face, there were none to be found. His face was as relentless as the glacier around them, though the remains of Jonesy and Scott still clung to his cheeks, dried to a red-brown crust.

The Winoquin didn't bother forming their gauntlet of flesh. Broken and clinging to each other, Ezra and Stu made their way to the fire, their heads held high, their chests burning with love. The Winoquin filed in around them, joining the circle as the summer grasses smoldered and emitted a pitiful amount of heat. The temperature had dropped considerably.

They sat on the frozen surface of the glacier, angling their eyes so they didn't have to see the stale bloodstains of their friends' corpses. The elder sat, studying them, as Maq sat next to them.

The elder's thin lips began to dance, and Maq narrated his ballet.

"The spirits speak, tell us not to slay the orca, but to give chase. If an orca dies while being chased, it is not the Winoquin's fault. If the orca survives, it may go. It was meant to be."

Stu and Ezra sat in silence, trying to understand the elder's metaphor.

"You're going to chase us?" Ezra asked.

"Not both, just you, Ezra. There is a place on the glacier, more sacred than even the grounds we sit upon. I have seen this place, for I am the elder. If you make it to this place, you are considered sacred, and no harm will befall you. We will help you. But if you should fall, we feast . . . on two."

"Why do I have to go?" Ezra asked.

"He must record the ritual, ensure our prosperity. When the ice is gone, we can replay the ritual, keep ourselves going."

Stu looked to Ezra, noted the dark circles around his eyes, the way, even though it was freezing out, his sweaty hair clung to his forehead. Infection setting in. He glanced down at Ezra's feet, cold and blue, freezing on the ice.

Stu began untying his boots.

"It is your birthday," Maq translated. "As such, you may ask a wish, for a day of birth is a special day. Make it a good one; don't throw it away."

Ezra looked at Stu, a thought skittering across his mind. *Don't kill Stu.* But he knew this was not the wish he should ask for, knew it would be denied and his wish would be rejected.

"Where is this sacred space?" Ezra finally asked.

Maq stood then, pointed to the upturned tear in the distance, the snow-covered mountain whose buried soil hadn't seen the sun in thousands of years. It pointed up at the sky, jagged and hidden underneath a blanket of snow.

Ezra nodded.

"On the side of the mountain, there is a place, a hollow, an old place of power. This is the birthplace of the Winoquin; from this place we all sprang. When our elder dies, we gather here, and we race. The first person to reach the cave becomes the new elder, guided by the spirits."

"I'll go," Stu said. "Ezra can record."

Maq spoke to the elder.

The elder shook his head, gave back a retort.

"The spirits were clear. They have talked to this one, marked him out. It is his birthday, a sacred day, the day his ancestors come to visit. He must be the one who goes."

"It's ok," Ezra said, his voice weak, as if his vocal cords themselves were trying to conserve energy.

Stu kicked his boots off, thankful he could provide some comfort to Ezra. "Take these."

Ezra tried to put them on with one hand, stomping his feet into them. Stu knelt and told Ezra to lift his foot, the Winoquin looking on in quiet contemplation. When the boots were on, Stu began tightening the laces, knotting them so they wouldn't come undone as Ezra ran for his life.

"For my birthday wish, I would like, a three-hour head start."

Maq relayed this information, and the elder nodded.

"You have until the sun reaches its low-point. Then we come."

Ezra nodded, and Stu ran back to the ice hut, the Winoquin watching him cautiously, their hands never far from their spears.

He returned with a blanket and threw it over Ezra's shoulders. Then he turned Ezra to face him, pressed his lips against Ezra's cold mouth, and they kissed deep and hard, Winoquin be damned.

When they pulled apart, they found the Winoquin, every single one of them, staring up at the sun, watching its dull luminescence as it burned in the sky.

"Run," Stu whispered, pressing his forehead to Ezra's.

"We could just die," Ezra said. "Die together."

"Run!" Stu shouted, shoving Ezra along. He looked over his shoulder, hurt and stumbling.

Stu charged at him. "Ruuuunnn!" he roared, and Ezra broke into a trot.

Watching his lover flee, Stu stood among the Winoquin, his bare feet standing in the red slush where they had devoured Jonesy.

He stood that way, watching as Ezra made his way up the

glacier, crunching across it in Stu's boots. For three hours, he stood that way, his feet turning blue.

When the Winoquin dropped their eyes from the sun, they picked up their spears with the dreamlike movements he'd seen before. They plodded away, their spears tipped to the skies, unlit birthday candles to celebrate Ezra's first day on Earth, on a day which might wind up being his last. Stu bent down and picked up his camera, following the Winoquin, hoping for the glacier to open up underneath them and swallow them whole.

CHAPTER 16
THE GIFT OF THE KULAJACK

EZRA RAN, despite the pain in his body. Despite his burned face and chest, the wetsuit still fused to his skin, Ezra ran... because he wasn't just running for himself, not anymore. He ran for two, for himself and Stu.

If he had just been running for himself, he would have given up and fallen to the ice, waiting for the Winoquin to find him, plunge their spears into him, and feast on his meat. But he was running for two, so that wasn't an option. Even if it meant the death of him, even if his arms fell off and his legs came off like that one knight in *Monty Python and the Holy Grail*, he would keep going. "It's just a flesh wound," he hissed as he ran, his legs and arms pumping.

The further up the glacier he went, the colder it grew. He'd thought it was cold before, but he didn't know real cold until he climbed up and up, the frigid air falling off the slope of the mountain and splashing across his face.

With each step, he expected to plunge into a hidden crevasse. In his mind, he hoped the death would be quick, that he wouldn't fall to the bottom of some icy abyss, and land perfectly fine, forcing him to climb out of the pit with his maimed hand.

The ground crunched underneath him, and fifteen minutes into his jog, he found himself stumbling along like a drunk, like that first time he and Stu had hooked up outside some Tulsa bar after another powwow. On Sundays, they always left early. All the good shit was done by then. As soon as night fell, Stu and Ezra, and the other members of the crew, would disappear to the nearest bar. That night, despite the drinking prowess of Jonesy, they had remained at the table even though their flight out of town was early the next day; they were determined to outlast Jonesy . . . a feat of endurance if ever there was one. Jonesy had packed it in around one in the morning. Last call was at one-thirty, and then they'd stumbled up the street to the Hilton. Ezra had thought to drop Stu off at the door and make his way to his own room, but as he'd turned to leave, Stu's hand had snaked out, grabbed a handful of his shirt, and pulled him inside his room.

They missed their flight the next day, their phones ringing as Jonesy and Scott had texted them, wondering where they were. They both pleaded hangovers, paid for their rooms out of their own pockets, and spent the next day falling in love, while also actually dealing with hangovers. Nothing could bring a relationship closer than stale alcohol breath and room service in the morning. Nothing . . .

Although, almost dying together on a glacial surface might come in a close second.

His boots crunched ice, and he went away, fell into a stupor of physical exertion, the best way to be when your body was actively dying. Ezra went away, traveled to the back of his mind, disconnected himself from his flesh.

The ice cracked and grumbled, and his legs burned almost as bad as his chest and face.

Running for two . . . running for two. He thought the words, set them to the beat of his roaring heart, the crunch of the ice beneath him, and onward he ran, his mind falling into a trance, the ice hurtling by.

As he climbed the gentle slope of the glacier, the teardrop mountain loomed above, its tip brushing the bottoms of gray clouds.

He hoped for snow, hoped for something that would hide his tracks, make him harder to find. He was under no delusions he could outrun the Winoquin, knew all it would take was one turned ankle, or complete exhaustion to overcome him, and he would be dead—*they* would be dead.

The wind sang to him, kissed his earlobes with an acid sting, whispered the songs of the Winoquin in his ears. *Cold waters, warm hearts. Death for life, death for life.*

Running for two . . .

In his trance-like state, with his feet pounding ice, a third

WE LIKE IT CHERRY

inhabited him, a spirit of some age, tied to the land, tied to the mountain. Pleased with his ascent, with the purity of Ezra's run, the spirit moved in, found it more exciting than anything it had encountered in some time. The genderless entity fingered Ezra's exhilaration gently, felt it in the place where its heart would be. It took up some of Ezra's space, kept his legs pumping long after Ezra should have fallen to the ground.

On and on it went, running for three now.

The spirit within, a reticent one who had been hurt during its last go-around, found once more the joy of living within this tortured man's breast. When the call came this next time, it wouldn't deny its rebirth as it had done for so many decades; it would be born again. Onward they ran, spirit, Ezra, and the love within.

Up the slope the spirit sprinted, moving Ezra's tortured flesh with the greatest of ease. The spirit didn't flag, its energy tireless. It ran over a field of broken ridges, as if the glacier had crashed into a great wall, crumpling up upon itself. Each ridge stood twenty feet high, the drop-off on the other side steep and dangerous.

But the spirit knew the ridges, had memorized each one over hundreds of years, dozens and dozens of cycles. The glacier changed, but did so slowly. Down the spirit went, picking out handhold and foothold with effortless ease. Up another ridge, down another slope, mimicking the spiked vertebrae of the char it had once feasted upon.

In the valley of one of these slopes, it came upon a group of creatures, their hair green, their eyes white as the glacier—the blinded race. They stood staring up at the sun, soaking up its cold bounty.

The spirit, so shocked by the appearance of this race, skidded to a stop, lost its grip upon the man it held, and then vanished into thin air as Ezra came forward, reestablished his identity.

Ezra screamed as his pain crashed into him once more, his voice cutting through his throat like a knife. The creatures turned toward him. Humanoid in nature, their skin was orange, layered in more green hair, or perhaps fur. To Ezra, they seemed almost catlike, their bodies lithe, their faces alien but wondrous.

Ezra felt the strain of his muscles, and he sat on the ground, falling like a suspended biology class skeleton with its supports cut. Puddled on the ground, the green-furred creatures swirled around him, and he quivered in his skin, though even those small tremors seemed to soak up the last of his energy.

One of the white-eyed things reached out to him, tentative, as scared as Ezra perhaps. It touched his head, throwing its own face back and up, staring at the sun with those blind eyes. It yowled, its voice twisting and bending in ways that made the flesh on Ezra's arms rise, another wasteful use of the last dregs of his energy.

The others of its kind circled around, flexing their fingers, their tails twitching in the air as the claws at the end of their fingertips retracted and extended in nervous anticipation. A green tongue, kelp-like in nature, fell from the creature's mouth, reached out, caressed Ezra's face in a probing manner.

"I have to go," Ezra said, but his words were cut off as the tongue darted for his mouth. It entered him, cold and forceful, and he had the oddest sensation of being pulled inward, as if his entire being wanted to escape from his mouth. *This must be what a juice box feels like.*

The plant-like appendage pulled the life from him, made him disappear, and he fell away once more, to the back part of his consciousness. The tongue probed deeper, seemed to rip through his skin peeling away layers, and he felt its cold embrace around his heart.

It searched him, rifling through his soul the way the Canadian customs agents had rifled through his bag, pulling out his cigarettes, his I.D., all his clothes. It sorted through him, found his flaws, his need to be loved, his need to replace the love he'd lost when his father had denied him and his mother had done nothing about it. It learned of his pride, of his hubris. It encountered his disdain for who he was, and then finally, it settled onto the core of him, the love he felt for Stu. On this part, it lingered, spinning and studying Ezra's heart as his flesh continued to suck inward.

Without warning, the creature pulled back, glared at him with those empty eyes, so white, so wet. His own horrid reflection glared back at him from those opaque orbs.

The being made noises, words maybe, more likely sensations, and the others of its kind gathered around him, their kelp-tongues escaping from their mouths, moving as if they had a life of their

WE LIKE IT CHERRY

own, as if the vaguely humanoid creatures were but vessels for these alien green tentacles, their ends rough, covered in shining bulbs, the kelp flesh glowing a light yellow. The tentacles latched to Ezra—his neck, his cheek, his eye, his mouth. His body went rigid as if being jolted by a thousand volts all at once . . . and he went away once more.

From above, the spirit of the Winoquin, hungry for life once more, waited to see what would happen. The kulajack left the outsider lying prone on the ice. They'd sought him out, found him pure, which was good. The spirit knew the Winoquin and the kulajack held an ancient feud. One hunting the other, and the other hunting in return. They had no need to encounter each other any longer, but the feud ran deep. The truce still held, but it could always go bad. At some point in the past, the two groups realized their feud had destroyed their peoples. Now, they stayed out of each other's way, the kulajack keeping to the inhospitable realms of the glacier, the Winoquin existing on the periphery of the icy expanse.

The spirit, who had once slain a whale by itself when it was a man named Flurk, knew about long odds, knew the other spirits weren't rooting for this broken man, this burned husk. But the spirit liked long odds, knew it could help, so when the kulajack disappeared, melting into the ice, it slipped into the man, Ezra, the name strange and foreign.

It tumbled through the man's memories. This was not like slipping into the mind of one of the Winoquin, because there you knew everything. From the land of the dead, they kept watch over the people, for they were all one and the same, fathers, mothers, sisters, brothers, grandparents, stretching out to the beginning of time, to when the world birthed them upon the land, spitting them out as one, thrusting them out onto the glacier and letting them fend for themselves. And they had, fighting the cold, fighting the beasts that roamed the ice, those once larger, stranger, deadlier.

But all those creatures, with the exception of the kulajack, had gone the way the Winoquin were heading. And maybe that was a good thing. Maybe that was the way they were meant to be. Perhaps the Winoquin had lasted longer than they should have. Perhaps the last ritual had been ill-fated, and the ritual before that even more so.

In Ezra's mind, the spirit found things of wonder, things none of the Winoquin had ever dreamed of or imagined. A world built tall, a world where a man could wear pants that exposed his shins and calves all year long. A world where a man could climb into metal, ride the sky like a bird. The Winoquin were not made for this, didn't need this.

But in this man's memories, he found other things, signs the Winoquin were on their way out. The glaciers were disappearing. The polar bears, long their brothers, were dying out. The heat was coming, and the land of their birth would disappear. It wasn't the earth that gave rise to the Winoquin, but the ice itself, grinding and chewing and eating up the land, turning it into something else, a cold heat that cooked the elements and spat out brown men and other beings. When Mother Ice went, they would go too, the milk of their creator having vanished along with the glaciers.

The spirits of the Winoquin, the detached wandering watchers, knew they could prolong their existence, but for what purpose? To become like the people below, the dirty impure people who bent the world to their whims so they didn't have to fight, so they didn't have to survive? Then they wouldn't be Winoquin at all, but something else, something unnatural.

The spirit picked up Ezra's body, felt the fresh energy running through it, a gift from the kulajack, as if they too knew extinction was the way things were going to go—better to hurry it along. If the glaciers went, so too would the kulajack. The ice was their food, the sun their play. Without the ice, they would perish.

The spirit guided Ezra up and down the ridges, around crevasses hidden underneath sheets of thin ice that had spread over the last winter. He guided the man's body, playing in his mind and shaking his head at all the wondrous things it beheld. But it was enough to behold them, enough to see the capabilities of the people from the south. The spirit shuddered at the thought of living among the southerners, in their land where survival was doled out in tedium, where food was earned by standing in one place, doing one thing over and over until you could barely stand it anymore. No, this was not the way, but still . . . they had some nice things.

Onward the spirit trudged, thankful for the energy infusion of the kulajack.

WE LIKE IT CHERRY

Ezra went for a ride, knowing his body had been hijacked, and he only existed as a whisper in the back of his mind. It was warm back there, the temperature unable to touch him, the pain of his tortured body unable to reach him. The only pain he felt was the absence of Stu Nofire, the Umatilla cameraman he had fallen in love with despite all odds.

As the glacial world slipped by him, he watched it as a movie, as a Netflix series he was bingeing on the couch, the only thing missing the embrace of Stu, the warmth of his hand, the smell of his skin, papery and musky at the same time. The show played on and on, a nature documentary of a desolate place bound to vanish in Stu's lifetime.

A shame. From the depths of his mind, watching the world slide by, watching knife-sharp ridges of ice descend and fall, hill after jagged hill, he learned to appreciate it, learned to see the telltale signs of life in the middle of nowhere. There a footstep, there some sort of bird with a long bill floating in the sky, the strange creatures who skittered out of the way at the approach of man, visible out of the corners of the screen, which were the corners of his eyes. Stu would like this show, would appreciate the cinematography, point out the golden shots, the ones where someone had risked their life and limb for the perfect picture, edging out onto a crystal spire that could crumble underneath them at any given moment.

He could have pressed forward, asserted his mind once more, but whatever was guiding him moved much faster than he would have, knew the land as if it had been born to it, which he supposed it had. So, he sat back on his mental couch and yearned, hoping Stu was having an easier time of it.

CHAPTER 17
LAYER BY LAYER

STU WALKED WHERE the Winoquin walked, trying to maintain his balance while recording his journey. Over his shoulder he wore a bag with extra batteries, extra memory cards. He didn't record everything, couldn't in most places as the land grew more rugged, rougher to traverse. Sometimes he had to stuff the camera in the bag, because he needed to use two hands to guide himself up and over the icy ridges, like the many rows of teeth in a shark's hungry maw, jutting up from the glacier's smashed jaw.

Sometimes he had to stop as the lens froze over, had to breathe on it and polish the glass with ultra-soft cloths designed for the task.

His feet were frozen now, the toes turning an uncomfortable shade of blue. He wondered how the Winoquin could still plod on, nearly naked but for the spots where their gear covered their skin, woven ropes and hooks made of bone. Their skin, so brown and cold it had turned purple, showed no signs of frostbite. Meanwhile, Stu could no longer feel his feet. But the deal was he had to keep walking, had to keep feeling, had to keep recording. If he went back on this, surely, they would kill him, maybe have Maq try and figure out how to run the damn thing . . . or whatever was controlling Maq. Wherever Maq was, he was no longer here.

The Winoquin paid as much attention to him as they did the sun above, meaning absolutely none. They trudged onward, their spears pointing to the sky, their indestructible feet pressing through the ice. They looked like regular people on a nature walk—nothing more, the way Ezra might look walking through the streets

WE LIKE IT CHERRY

of Los Angeles, stopping every now and then at a taco cart to get his fill. That motherfucker loved tacos.

Stu laughed at an image in his head, Ezra pounding tacos, eating with relish out front of a taco cart late at night, his head cocked to the side, juices running down his chin. He didn't have a particular favorite, would just eat any old thing slapped between two corn tortillas. Corn, he always insisted on corn. "Flour tortillas are for the white people," he said. Stu didn't know about that. He wasn't white, preferred flour, but he never corrected Ezra. He was the expert, the one who had tasted all the tacos Los Angeles had to offer. He never met a taco he hadn't liked, a double entendre they joked about with an embarrassing frequency.

Ahead the Winoquin disappeared, and Stu shouldered his camera, peered over the edge of the ridge, dreaded the descent. His feet, bare and beyond recovery, searched out footholds, which he tested by releasing his grip for a beat to see if he was going to fall or remain standing. In this painstaking manner, his skin sticking to the ice, he rose and fell with the Winoquin, leaving behind bits of skin he couldn't even feel. The glacier was skinning him alive, layer by layer.

Somewhere ahead, Ezra ran, his love, burned and exhausted, his mind not quite right. The further he went, the harder it would become. That they hadn't found him yet was something of a surprise to Stu. He kept expecting to come upon the Winoquin heading in the other direction, dragging Ezra behind them like a slaughtered seal, his blood painting the glacier as Jonesy's had, as Scott before him.

But after every ridge, onward they continued, climbing up and over, with nothing but the faint set of footprints on the glacier's surface to assure them that Ezra did, in fact, live.

On the north side of one ridge, the mountain hanging over them in the near distance, the Winoquin had stopped, were pointing out strange tracks in the ice. Stu was both thankful for a break and rueful. On one hand, he needed the rest. On the other hand, moving was all that was keeping him warm.

With his camera, he scanned the tracks, and noted the presence of four toes, rounded like a cat's.

"Are there mountain lions out here?" Stu asked Maq. But it wasn't Maq, so he didn't answer.

When he went to record the tracks, one of the Winoquin put a cold blue hand over his camera and shook his head, his white eyes glinting like ice in the sun for the moment. Stu let the camera drop to the side, understood the message. No recording. Why, he didn't know, but there was much he didn't know about the Winoquin, and unless he wanted to wind up with a spear in his guts, which could still happen, he had to play by their rules.

These sets of tracks were strange. Instead of four footprints, he found only two, as if the mountain lions had been running only on their back feet. He'd never heard of mountain lions this far north, but he wouldn't put it past them. The northern reaches of the world, the icy places, were barely studied, presumed to be dead zones, but Stu had seen differently, had been provided with proof otherwise.

His heart sank in his chest as he studied the paw prints, knew Ezra couldn't fight off mountain lions. But as the Winoquin continued onward, their study of the tracks at an end, Stu was pleased to see the paw prints led in a different direction than Ezra's tracks.

It was a small blessing, perhaps even a short-lived one, but he would take it. Maybe things were lining up for them out here. Maybe everything would be alright. Then he looked down at his toes, frozen blocks of flesh, feelingless. They would have to come off once this was all over.

Not enjoying the thought, he shouldered his camera and disappeared behind the safety of the eyepiece, recorded the Winoquin climbing up a thirtieth ridge, using their spears to steady themselves as they ascended. When the last tribesman reached the peak, Stu let his camera fall, thought about sitting on the ice and letting this all happen without him.

Exhaustion hit him then, the pain of being cold, muscles drained of all their energy. His stomach revolted, gurgling at him. He resisted the urge to stuff handfuls of snow into his mouth just to fill his stomach, knew doing so would lower his body temperature even further. Ezra was still out there, waiting for him somewhere. He had to be there, to fight, to help. Even if they died, he wouldn't care. At least they would do it together.

Now all he had to do was keep himself moving, kick his ass into gear. The first step was the hardest, harder than climbing the

WE LIKE IT CHERRY

mountain itself. But once he stumbled forward, he maintained his motion, scaled the next ridge, and then clambered down the other side, his camera hanging by its strap.

"I'm coming for you Ezra," he said, repeating the line over and over. His body was so cold now that his lungs, chilled by the glacier's frozen air, were incapable of sending out hot breath. His breath was invisible now, as if he wasn't breathing at all. This was the Winoquin land of the dead, and he was one of them.

CHAPTER 18
FRIENDS DON'T LIE

WITHIN THE DEPTHS of his mind, Ezra started receiving guests, appearing as milky white blobs, vaguely human in form, though the features on their faces shifted constantly, as if they couldn't decide what they wanted to look like. Their hair rose and fell, shortening, lengthening, sometimes disappearing altogether. They sat with him on his mental couch, kept him company.

He spoke with them, the Winoquin of the past, waiting to be born again, floating among the land of the dead, their home, their birthplace. They told him tales, simple in their construction, of the Winoquin's past, and regaled him with legendary hunts, the horrors of the glacier, the nightmares they had fought, overcome, and made extinct.

Among these tales, Ezra absorbed the meaning of the Winoquin, the culture, the reason behind their chosen way of life, discovered it was the same as always—continuance, posterity, preservation of the past so the present might thrive. In this way, the Winoquin were no different from anyone else on the planet. They contained within them the same set of emotions, the same feelings. The only thing they lacked was drive, the desire to make oneself better, to improve oneself.

When his guests peered into his life, probed his mind while he reclined on his mental couch, far away from the pain and exhaustion of his body, they invariably became stuck on the defining questions of his life.

"If you love him, why don't you announce it, scream it from the top of the world?"

WE LIKE IT CHERRY

"Because it's simply not done," Ezra answered in pure thought, the common language of spirit and those on the verge of death—universal it turns out.

"It is done, when you do it."

Knowing what he knew about the Winoquin, he couldn't hope to explain how the world worked, how if he announced himself as gay, he would lose fans, lose clout, lose lots of things. The Winoquin couldn't understand, because none of this mattered to them. Love was a different thing among the Winoquin, a shared, communal thing. When the men went on a hunt, sometimes they lay with each other. It was lonely on the ice—cold. The comfort of another's body, regardless of genital composition didn't matter to them. If it didn't hurt the tribe, it helped the tribe. The women too would share each other's beds, become closer because of it. Everywhere they were, the net of community raged among them, forged of freely given love and desire and respect.

"Your ways are strange, southerner," the spirits seemed to say.

"They are our ways."

"A shame."

"Shame isn't the half of it."

The other thing they questioned was his drive, his desire for notoriety.

"What good is this for people to know you?" they asked, unable to understand. "What purpose does it serve?"

For this, Ezra had no answer, and in the simple questions of the visitors—the intruders into his mind, who only stayed for a moment as there wasn't much room left in there—he found his world laid bare, the skin and fat carved away to expose the bones of his life. The things he had thought were complicated and unsolvable were actually quite simple from the perspective of the Winoquin spirits.

"What good is fame?" he mused to himself. "What good is being known if the person everyone knows isn't real?"

His life, his mistakes, were folly in the Winoquin's eyes. When the spirits departed, they left a lingering aura of sadness behind for the man so confused by the world he had denied love and freedom, had chosen to pretend to be something he wasn't for the sake of the riches he was promised, which weren't even riches when you held them in your hands. What good was someone recognizing you on the street when there was no one at home to tell the story to? What good were a million hits on YouTube, if no one at home liked what you made?

On the screen, the Winoquin in the driver's seat began climbing, leading Ezra's body up the ice-covered slope of the mountain. Here, the world was more treacherous, and not even the Winoquin, with its thousand-year understanding of the mountain, of the spirit path, could predict what would happen. But it certainly did a better job of climbing than Ezra would have.

Ezra maintained his own ascent, one of a different nature, a harsher one, more philosophical. Though it was a spiritual journey, it was no less dangerous. In his mind, he battled with himself, warred with who he had been. Through the Winoquin's simple questions, he grew unsure of himself, and his own self-loathing grew.

All this time—wasted. All the time he could have been living with Stu, making love to him, celebrating every moment of their life together, and he'd bagged it all, made Stu keep everything under wraps. Stu wasn't embarrassed, didn't care if Ezra had a dime, didn't give a fuck if he lived in a shack or a mansion. But Ezra cared what people thought of him, cared too much, had sacrificed the truth of himself for the lies of someone else.

On the screen, a cold blue hand grasped an outcropping of ice affixed to cold, gray stones underneath. The view rose up to meet the hand as the ancient Winoquin rose upward, but then the ice crumbled, and the Winoquin tumbled to the ground, landing with a hard thud that echoed through the surround-sound of Ezra's mental living room.

"Sounded like it hurt."

Ezra didn't like hurt, had avoided it ever since his dad . . . ever since his dad had disowned him, called him a faggot and an embarrassment. That pain, that life-defining pain, had surrounded him, woven a cocoon of hurt and anger around his core, and though he could have escaped it, broken free, no longer a slithering, fuzzy caterpillar, he refused the metamorphosis, clung to his cocoon, hidden behind strands of silk—the lies he'd told to the world about who he was and what he stood for.

Inside, a beautiful beast hid, glorious, the markings on its wings unique, the reality of him, but he refused to show it because the world was a cold, harsh place. The world, the one below, not this passive, icy paradise, but the world down south, had no love for him, would see his markings and make fun of them or try and place a net over him, throw him in a kill jar and pin him down with miniscule steel pins.

Better to stay in the cocoon, or so he'd thought.

The Winoquin, in their world devoid of social constructions, had peeked inside him, told him he was beautiful and should abandon his cocoon. But it was too late now. Far too late.

Where had they been when he needed them? Where were they when he was being asked to come up here in the first place? That was the most damning thing of all, that had he not agreed to come here, he would still be down below, among the liars and the pretenders, playing his part, an actor playing the role of a lifetime, sunk into it because that's the only way he could avoid the pain, avoid seeing someone he loved snarling in his face, spittle flying from his mouth as his lower lip gathered behind his teeth to force out the first consonant sound of the word that had cut him in two and left him drifting alone in the world—until he'd found Stu.

The unfairness of it all rankled him, made his comfy, cozy sofa of consciousness less so. The stupidity of himself—a hard thing to see. Though he tried to distract himself with the screen, his anger grew and grew until he could no longer lounge.

At that moment, a dark shape sailed by his corporeal head and embedded itself in the ice wall to his left.

The spirit turned, regarding the others below. The Winoquin had caught up to him somehow. Their milky eyes glared up at him, their arms cocked back like Olympic javelin throwers, and Ezra, through the filter of the Winoquin spirit's eyes, beheld the beings within the living Winoquin.

He sat up on his mental couch, surged forward in rage, displacing the spirit who had helped him.

He wouldn't allow it to be the cause of his death, forced himself to take his life in his own hands. The spirit dissipated, and Ezra came forward, stepped into the hell of his body. His hands ached, each flex of his fingers threatening to snap his stiff fingers in two. His back was on fire, as were his legs and thighs, the burn in them worse than the burning of his chest, the sting of the wind upon his singed face.

The mountain before him, covered in ice for as long as the spirits could recall, rose before him, a great canine tooth, cracked and jagged on the west side, smooth and unscalable on the east. Its dark rocks gave the ice a gray hue. Each grip of long-frozen ice sent pain through his hands. That was good. He still felt them, at least.

A spear clanged off the icy rocks to his right, clattered to the ground, and then tumbled downward. Ezra pressed himself against the rocks, his burnt chest scraping along the ice, deceptively smooth to look at, but rough against his ruined chest.

The seal-fur blanket around his shoulders, which had kept him from dying, became a burden, and he tossed it to the ground. His head swam as he went up and up, taking risks he never would have just a few days ago. He leaped from ice shelf to ice shelf, sailing through the air, weightless for a moment. A tortured scream escaped his lips, only for the wind to snatch it away. When he landed, he did so like one of those flying squirrels, his legs and arms splayed out in the air. His body thumped off the ice, and then his hands and feet scrambled for purchase to keep him from plummeting down the mountain face. Then he'd stand up again, keep probing the surface as spears, knocked off target by the wind, clattered off the frozen mountainside.

The wind became his friend, one of those friends you always dread having around because they know who you are and don't sugarcoat a damn thing. With its cutting gale, it slapped him across the face, told him to keep moving, guarded him from the errant throws of the Winoquin. Meanwhile, it whispered the harsh truths of his life in his ears.

You wasted all this time.
You were scared.
You're a coward.
It's too late.

His hands grew blocky and uncoordinated, his fingers little more than frozen bones encased in thickened flesh. They didn't react the way he wanted them to, and he spoke back to the wind. "Help me."

The wind whipped around him, swirling the unburnt remains of his hair about his face. Chunks of ice and snow broke free from the tooth of the world, battered him about the face. Above, the wind swirled, turning into a massive snow devil, spinning and spinning. Its base reached down to the Winoquin, blinding them as they tried in vain to send their spears through Ezra's back.

He mounted another ice shelf, stood staring at a sheer sheet of icicles hanging like fangs. He thought to break them off, throw them down at the Winoquin, kill them the way they were trying to kill him . . . but if he did that, all would be lost. This was their home, their rules, so he bypassed the fangs, searched for another way up.

Above, the snow devil had expanded, reached the heavens. The gray clouds above ripped apart, shredding like a thin layer of cotton. The sun kissed him with its pale light, made him squint his eyes as ice crystals spun around him.

You're almost there.
No rest now.
To rest is to die.

The wind spurred him on, and finding reserves of energy he didn't know he had, he jammed his hands into the ice, cracked through the surface, splitting his knuckles in the process of gouging his own handholds. He rose upward, hugging the mountainside, scraping the burnt skin over his heart against the cool surface of the mountain. Screams and grunts of pain escaped his lips, animalistic cries.

Somewhere below him was the reason he did this. Somewhere below him stood Stu, the man he'd wronged.

Career over love.
Ha!

The wind laughed in his ear, the truth-telling friend ever to the end.

His arms strained until he thought his biceps were going to tear clean off the bone. His thighs pushed, and his calves ached. Up he went, the sun pouring down upon him, bringing him the faintest bit of heat, offering the faintest bit of hope.

The spears continued to fall around him, some so caught up in the wind that they landed sideways. One of these caught him across the back of the legs, and he flinched, lost his grip, then lost fingernails as he dug his hands into ice, delaying the fall and keeping himself from plummeting down the side of the mountain.

He gritted his teeth and continued to scale the mountain one hand at a time, whipped by the wind and the words it whispered.

Promises filled his mind, each one a mini-deal, a promise to be better to himself and to everyone. *If you get me out of this, I promise no more pretending, no more lying to myself or others. If you get me out of this, I promise I won't care about my job or lack of success. If you get me out of this, I will be thankful for everything I have.*

Ezra didn't know who "you" was, could only hope whoever it was listened, had some measure of pity within it for the crimes he'd done to himself and to his lover.

From above, there came a great cracking sound. Whoever was listening clearly didn't care. A shelf of ice and snow broke, came tumbling down upon him, smothering his body in an icy grave.

"Fuck you," Ezra managed to say just as he brought his arm up over his head.

CHAPTER 19
STU'S TRIBE

STU STOOD AT the bottom of the tooth of the world, looking upward at a small, dark blob. *That's Ezra. He's almost there.*

Gritting his teeth, Stu studied his feet. He was missing a toe now, had lost it during the last climb over the ridges. His blood didn't flow from it though. He was too cold for that to happen.

Above him, the Winoquin climbed, their spears in their hands, their heads tilted upward.

It occurred to Stu that he had to do something. He had to put the camera down, to become part of the world. He should have done this a long time ago, stopped using the lens as a filter for life. He could have told Ezra how he felt, could have demanded he declare their love publicly so they could start living their life together. But he couldn't. He was the camera man. He didn't make decisions, didn't call the shots. He was a leaf floating on the pond of life at the mercy of the water, the wind, and the pond's more active denizens.

But if he had done it. If he had delivered the ultimatum, they wouldn't be in this mess to begin with. They wouldn't be thousands of miles from home, losing body parts, getting scarred and maimed, on the verge of being eaten by people they couldn't argue with. If he had put the camera down, he would be . . . dead.

He held the camera up, looked at it, brought the eyepiece up to his eye. He tilted it upward, peering through the spinning haze of the mountain, its own snowy environment, raging and angry despite the sun. The wind kicked up. He zoomed in. Watched as a spear just missed Ezra. He panned down, studied the Winoquin strung out on the side of the mountain. Without the camera, they might kill him . . . maybe.

He pulled the camera down, then took his first step forward. He could no longer tell if he was simply cold or experiencing pain. It seemed the two sensations weren't all that dissimilar when you broke it down.

You're not hurt. You're just cold.

He repeated the words in his mind, began his ascent. He moved recklessly, the camera held in one hand, while he used the other to steady himself as he climbed. The Winoquin moved easily on the side of the mountain, as if they knew every particular nook and cranny. He followed their path, found it easier.

Ahead of him, one of the Winoquin reached up with a steady hand, tireless, and Stu grabbed him by the foot, pulled him from the ledge. The man fell, tumbling down below, rolling past Stu, his movements too slow and deliberate to stop his descent. Despite all that had happened, Stu hoped he hadn't seriously injured the man. He was just doing what he had to do.

Up and up he went, pulling the Winoquin from ledges and perches, sending them crashing down below. Leaving behind bits of skin and a stream of swear words, Stu ascended again and again.

The Winoquin never looked back, had no concept of needing to check out what was going on behind them. They were oblivious, focused only on one thing: their precious ritual, the extension of their tribe's being. But Stu couldn't worry about that, though he felt sorry for them. He had one tribe, a tribe of his choosing, a tribe that only numbered two, and he wouldn't let his go extinct either. Him and Ezra, the only tribe he ever needed. So, he understood the Winoquin's needs and desires to continue, but it was no match for his own drive. The Winoquin had had centuries. He and Ezra had only had three years.

As he wrapped a cold hand around another ankle, he yanked, sending a man crashing down below. His body cracked on the rocks and stopped moving. As Stu watched, the whites of his eyes unclouded, and he stared into the face of a dead Winoquin. *A shame.*

The wind howled, pelting him with dislodged chunks of ice and snow. He squinted into the dull glare of the sun as he climbed upward. His body no longer sweated, didn't seem to be a body at

WE LIKE IT CHERRY

all—more like a hunk of frozen meat he commanded. Sometimes, the body listened, sometimes it did its own thing, as when he tumbled down a slope, landing next to a Winoquin who was just picking himself up. Stu thought he was in for a fight, but the Winoquin paid him no attention.

Stu filmed the man's face, his clouded eyes, then turned and rushed to climb back up the mountain before the man.

As he climbed, Stu gained ground with the speed of one who was about to lose everything. The Winoquin plodded onward in their inevitability. They had always been here, would always be here. This, they were assured.

When the avalanche hit, Stu pressed his face forward, hid underneath an outcropping of rock and ice. As far as avalanches went, it could have been worse. As the wave of white death flowed past him, he turned and watched it whisk away many of the tribesmen behind him.

The tooth of the world was hungry, made many men a meal on that day. When the sound of tumbling ice had faded away, he stepped out and surveyed the mountain above. The mountainside had changed. Five Winoquin were ahead of him, but there was no Ezra, not that he could see, anyway.

The Winoquin in the lead stopped where Stu had last seen Ezra—Maq, his arms thick, his belly rounder than the others—lifted his spear in the air, began jabbing it into the snow.

He's buried.

Stu put on his last burst of speed, perhaps the last he'd ever have in this world, and he climbed upward. The camera still recorded—fields of snow and ice, buried limbs jutting out of them, the flesh turning blue, the muted sun above, beaming down upon them with mock heat, the swirling wind, and the panting of Stu as he continued muttering, "You're not hurt; you're just cold."

CHAPTER 20
THE TOOTH OF THE WORLD

EZRA SUFFOCATED SLOWLY under the weight of the ice too great to break through. It pinned him down like a school bully, icy knees on his arms, its full weight on his torso.

When he opened his eyes, blackness.

When he opened his mouth to scream, it filled with snow.

When he tried to breathe through his nose, the snow fluttered into his nasal passages.

His body fought, it strained against his cruel tormenter, but the tormenter didn't budge an inch.

Ezra retreated to the couch, backed away from the screen of his life. *The TV's busted. Nothing on there but darkness. Must've lost the signal.*

But not completely.

The spirit, the one who had dragged Ezra across the glacier, halfway up the mountain, appeared once more, drawn by the man's willingness to fight for his life. It didn't understand all that happened in the man's mind. Didn't understand about taxes or fame or reality TV, but Ezra would have made a good Winoquin.

The spirit, freed of the fear of death, calmed the body, moved in little spurts, down and up, creating a hair's width of space with each subtle movement of Ezra. Little by little, the space it created as it crushed the ice crystals and snow below allowed it create even more space. It didn't feel the cold, didn't fear suffocation. It could go on like this for days . . . it was already dead after all.

WE LIKE IT CHERRY

By the time Stu reached the snowy landing where Ezra had disappeared, the Winoquin were all standing around, plunging their spears into the snow, searching for Ezra's body. One of the Winoquin lifted its spear into the air and over its head, winding up with maximum power.

Stu reached up, the camera dangling from a strap, and he slipped the spear out of the man's hands. When the Winoquin's hands came down empty, he stood looking at them, trying to figure out what had happened.

Stu sent the tip of the spear through the back of the man's neck, the tip erupting from his throat before he pulled it back. Blood splattered the ice, dripping thick like syrup upon the ground. The Winoquin turned to him, began wrestling with the spear, seemingly oblivious of the mortal wound in its throat. As the life drained from the Winoquin and he fell to the ground, Stu let go of the spear and moved to the next man, waited for him to raise his spear in the air. As he'd done before, he plucked the weapon from this man's hands and opened up another throat. He then drove the spear through the man's eye for good measure. The tribesman jittered at the end of the weapon and fell to the ground, his one good eye turning a deep brown.

Below, Stu felt the snow shift. The remaining three Winoquin were busy on a different part of the landing, making spear-shaped holes in the snow and ice. Stu squatted; he knew the other Winoquin were digging their way out of the snow below and would soon start climbing. His hands, frozen and cold, scraped against the hard ice, the crystals like a thousand knives against his skin. He dug like a dog, bent over, his scooped hands flinging ice between his legs. Snot dripped from his nose, tears from his eyes. *So close. I'm so close. I can feel him here.*

His numb hands encountered resistance, and he dug with fury, uncovering the darkened remnants of a wet suit. Stu's hands flew, everything forgotten, the toe that had broken off, the flesh of his friends digesting in his belly, the camera dangling around his neck, the memory cards filled with nightmares. All he knew was his one reason for existing lay cold and buried under ice. He scooped an armful of slush off Ezra's face, and then he backed away, his butt skidding across the ice.

Those aren't Ezra's eyes. He was greeted by the milky orbs of a possessed Winoquin. His shock fell away, and a great, flaming anger consumed him. He dove back into the hole he'd dug, settled onto Ezra's chest, and began shaking his body.

"Get out of him, you son of a bitch. Get out!" With each syllable, he picked the body up and shoved it back down, Ezra's skull packing the ice underneath. "Get out!"

Ezra's heart fluttered in his chest as the screen went from black to daylight in a single second. Then, wonder of wonders, he found his favorite face peering back at him. Something about his face must have bothered Stu, because he scrambled back, a look of revulsion in his features. Ezra tried to sit up, to move forward and take control of the ship, but the spirit in the seat didn't seem to want to leave, and then Stu was on top of him, ragdolling his body.

Ezra pushed forward, using his love for that grimacing, grunting face as a crowbar to pry the spirit away from the controls. It departed without a goodbye. Ezra reached up one of his cold, tired hands, and placed it on the side of Stu's cheek, which was no different temperature-wise from the snow and ice.

Stu leaned down, placed his dry cracked lips against Ezra's own, and they kissed, the wind swirling ice around them. Ezra could have stayed like that for days, but then Stu was pulling away. "You have to go," he said. "Now!"

Stu pulled Ezra from his icy tomb, dragged him to his feet. For a moment, Ezra caught sight of Stu's frozen feet, was about to say something, and then Stu shouted at him, "Don't worry about me. Go! It's the only way."

Ezra nodded, looked upward, and saw a route he could take. He would continue his climb. Behind him, he heard Stu rushing through the snow, yelling and cursing. Ezra cast a look over his shoulder, saw Maq and a couple of other Winoquin headed in his direction. The blank look on their faces and their milky eyes were all he needed to see.

He ran and jumped at the side of the mountain, grunting as he contacted the unforgiving ice and the stone underneath. Like a spider, he scrambled, pushing his weight upward, expecting a spear in the back at any moment.

"No!" Stu shouted below, and then the sound of more scuffling.

WE LIKE IT CHERRY

Ezra crawled foot by foot up the side of the mountain, the wind howling, the sun shining down in his eyes as he looked upward. He must have been a third of the way up the mountain. Wherever the Winoquin's sacred place was, he hoped it wasn't much further. Seeing Stu had reenergized him, seeing him hurting had panicked him, but the human body can only take so much. Sooner or later, he would die on the side of this mountain, left like one of the climbers on Mount Everest. At least there, they had guests every now and then as other, luckier ascendants passed by.

Here, no one visited, except for the Winoquin when conditions were right. But hey, climate change was real, right? He'd only be frozen for like another ten or fifteen years if he died. The thought didn't reassure him, and as he wondered what it would be like to be frozen alive, he fell into something that shocked him, took his breath away—warmth.

His skin, so used to the cold, began to tingle, the sensation not dissimilar from the pins and needles one feels after standing up and finding your foot has fallen asleep. Then came the itching and the burning, maddening as his skin came alive in the balmy, heat of . . . something.

As Ezra recovered from the shock of the temperature change, he grew aware of a dark cave in front of him. The heat seemed to emanate from within. As he walked closer, the ice that had accumulated in his hair and on his face turned back into water. His thirst was so great, he slurped these small droplets from his own skin.

He turned around, wondering if this was the place the elder had talked about, or if he had to go deeper into the cave. Rather than risk it, Ezra stumbled forward into the darkness, his body shambling as slow and deliberate as one of the possessed Winoquin. It was the only way he could make his tormented body move.

Even then, he was forced to push himself from rock outcropping to rock outcropping, half-jogging from spot to spot, leaning on the rocks to hold himself up.

When he glanced over his shoulder, he saw the spear tip of one of the Winoquin jutting up over the ledge.

Deeper into the blackness, he traveled.

At first, the darkness enveloped him, and then gradually, the cave filled with light. The source was dim to begin with, and then he saw them, faces and shapes in the gloom, the translucent spirits of the Winoquin. He walked among them a foreigner, bowing his head in their presence, for they would know more than he ever would, and one of them—he didn't know which—had helped him.

The Winoquin bowed back at him, recognized him for the survivor he was. Their thoughts rang through Ezra's mind as if they spoke out loud. "Welcome," they seemed to say. "You've done well to get here. Just a little further."

Behind him, he heard the scrape of feet on bare stone, followed by the clatter of a whalebone spear against rocks just to his right. He felt the wind of it; would have died if he'd leaned a few inches to his right at that moment.

"You're a survivor," the Winoquin said. "Not one of us by blood. But one of us by heart."

Ezra wasn't buying it, but that was part of survival, right? Always being ready? Always pretending something was too good to be true, even when it wasn't.

He splashed into a liquid so warm it seemed to burn his skin. By the hazy white light of the spirits, he lifted the water into his palms, felt its thickness, the viscosity of runny eggs as it slipped from his hands in snot-like gobs.

"Drink," the spirits seem to say.

Ezra did, the pungent liquid sliding down his throat, hanging off his uvula before dripping down the back of his esophagus. The flavor was rich and thick, not good, but not bad either. It coated his throat and his stomach, and the warmth of the fluid spread through his body. The things that hurt, stopped; the parts that didn't hurt thrummed with energy. He took another drink of the thick liquid.

"Not too much," the spirits warned. Such was the way with survival. Sometimes, too much of a good thing could kill.

He stepped back, waded to the edge of the pool, his eyes adjusting to the white light.

Maq stood there, a handful of other Winoquin behind him. As

he passed, they bowed their heads, closed their milky white eyes. When they lifted their heads, the light had gone from their eyes, and they stood as nothing more than tribesman on the edge of the world.

"You made it," Maq said, his voice neither happy nor sad, merely reporting the news as it were.

Ezra brushed past the Winoquin, left the cave, his body singing with heat and energy. At the ledge, he found Stu trying to climb upward, the camera in his hand. Ezra bent down and pulled him up. They embraced, too overcome by emotion to say anything. Touch was their language, their arms entwined around each other.

The Winoquin appeared, led by Maq. "You must go," Maq said. "We are done. You carry the strength of your tribe within you. You are the elder for your people."

"My tribe?" Ezra asked as he pulled back from Stu.

"I'm your tribe," Stu said.

"Go," Maq commanded. "This place will not last long. We are called to the next place."

Ezra had no time to ask what Maq was talking about. The Winoquin turned and walked back to the cave as the earth shook with a force that knocked Ezra and Stu from their feet. Above, the tip of the tooth of the world broke free, slid down the eastern side of the mountain. Another small tremor rocked the ground as Ezra's tribe stood.

"We need to get out of here," Stu said.

"Can you make it?" Ezra asked.

"I don't know."

The glacier screamed then, and from the slope above, a chunk of ice slid down, as large as a semi-truck. It crashed down in front of the entrance to the great cave, sealing the Winoquin inside.

"Does it matter?" Stu asked.

"I guess not."

Together, they began their descent, gripping crumbling ice and sliding down slick sides as the world rumbled beneath them and the glacier screamed.

The cold overtook Stu as they reached the bottom of the mountain. Ezra, his wounds much healed since the cave, bent and picked up

Stu, carrying him on his back. Warmth thrummed in his veins, the strength of the world contained within. He sprinted across the glacial planes, leaping up and over the thick, knife-like ridges of the crumpled glacier, retracing the footsteps he could find. The tremors came fast and furious, cracks and fissures opening up all around them.

Time grew short, and with Stu slumped over his shoulder, he ran onward. The hours drifted by, time seeming to stand still as he focused on putting one foot in front of the other, the energy within gurgling in his belly. With each step, he expected the world to open underneath him, to swallow them whole as it had done to the other Winoquin, the ones Stu hadn't sent to their doom.

Ridge after frozen ridge he climbed, his energy never flagging.

When they reached the edge of the glacier, the elder stood there, his face still covered in blood. He stood, small and weak now, waved at them, a smile on his face, his age-browned teeth gleaming in the sunshine.

Ezra waved back, rushed past the man, and plunged into the water, gripping Stu as tight as possible. They hit the water with a loud smack, and Ezra, swimming for two, dragged Stu to a moored umiak, holding onto it with one hand while trying to keep Stu's head above water.

"I need you to wake up, Stu. Babe, I need you to wake up." He removed his hand from the boat, slapped Stu on the face as the glacier began to calve all around them, dropping house-sized chunks of ice into the water. Stu's eyes fluttered, and he screamed at the shock of the cold.

"I need you to climb into that boat," Ezra said. "It's the last thing you need to do, and then we'll go home."

Stu's eyes fluttered some more, and Ezra kissed him on the lips, feeling some of his energy leaving him, entering Stu. His lover gasped and threw his head back as Ezra's lips dragged along the stubble of his throat. Stu's arms came up, gripped the lip of the boat, and attempted to haul himself into the vessel with Stu pushing him from underneath. Dripping, Stu fell into the boat and collapsed on the bottom, shivering.

Another chunk of ice the size of a large hill dropped into the water to the west, sending violent ripples out, making Ezra and the boat bob up and down. Eventually, he pulled himself aboard. With

WE LIKE IT CHERRY

frozen hands, he found the oars and began pulling them away from the deteriorating glacier.

When they were a safe distance away, he bent down and pulled the camera strap up and over Stu's unconscious head. He fumbled with it for a few moments, and then filmed as the great shelf of ice, the Winoquin land of the dead, slipped into the water, chunk by frozen chunk, as if someone had tipped up the far edge of Tolby Island.

When the world went silent, and the surface of the water went still, Ezra scrambled around in the boat, bent to the oars, and headed south, as far as he could tell.

"Not one of us by blood. But one of us by heart."

EPILOGUE
A NIGHT AT THE AWARDS

THE AUDIENCE APPLAUDED. One man stuck two fingers in his mouth and whistled so sharply Ezra winced. Cheers enwreathed him as he strolled to the stage, his ears burning red, his throat dry.

He took the steps slowly, lest he trip over them. They were tricky, their polished surface hard to perceive as they reflected the bright lights above into his eyes. He made it on stage with no great trouble. Later, when Stu would replay the moment for him on his phone, the tines of his hook hand tapping against its glassy surface, Ezra would be impressed by the calm he exuded.

But right then, in that moment, he didn't know what he was going to say. He stepped up to the podium, the A-list celebrities bowing to him and sliding backwards, disappearing like theater curtains after he shook their hands and balanced the award in his hand.

He turned and faced the crowd, setting the prize on the podium, his hands gripping its edge so he wouldn't fall, as if squeezing it tight could prevent his head from swimming into oblivion. Has anyone ever fainted up here? Anyone?

The sea of faces smiled at him, the applause died away, and he leaned forward, leveling his lips with the microphone. "I'd like to thank everyone who saw the value in this film, all the people who went on this journey with us. But most of all, I'd like to thank the Winoquin people for their hospitality. I've heard some ask, 'How can you forgive them?' And to that I answer, 'I can't.' But what I can do is move on. In that respect, I'm lucky. Some of my other colleagues are not. I'd like to take this moment to honor the memory of my producer Scott Mortensen, and my sound designer Matt Jones. I think about them every day."

I see them being eaten in my dreams.

"I'd like to thank Stu, who made it out with me, not all in one piece, but hey, we've still got the important bits."

The audience laughed sheepishly. *That was good. The joke was Stu's idea after all. Stu would rather have people laughing at him than pitying him.*

Stu smiled up at him, held up his hooks, and bowed his head from the wheelchair in the front row.

"I would like to thank the people who watched this documentary, and were able to look past the violence, the brutality, and find the commonality hidden within. *We Like It Cherry* isn't about cannibalism, spirits, or other worlds. In the end, it's about love, about being true to your tribe, whether they are family, either by blood or by choice. If you can take that lesson, and make your life better with that knowledge, then at least the loss of Scott, Jonesy, and the Winoquin men will have been worth something. Thank you for the recognition."

They applauded, and Ezra walked backstage, feeling empty, feeling like a sham. Success . . .

ACKNOWLEDGMENTS

I've never really done acknowledgments for a book of mine before. When I first started writing, it was a solo operation—writing, revising, editing, cover design (bad), marketing (none), and uploading all the files. I taught myself to do everything, more or less... sometimes less. So there was never anyone to thank, except for myself. And while I could still acknowledge myself, that would be weird and ignore all the people who had a hand in helping this book materialize out of the ether and into reality.

Despite what I said before, I will be thanking myself... sort of. By that, I mean I'd like to thank my subconscious. I'm sure there's a revolt taking place in there, as evidenced by the dream I had that inspired this novel. Somewhere in the depths of my mind, my ancestors exist, and they are not happy with me. In fact, they lured dream-me to a remote glacier and lit me on fire. Joke's on you, ancestors! You can't hurt me in my dreams, and I turned you into a novel.

In addition to the murderous spectres of my ancestors, I have to thank all the lovely Weirdos who supported me when I was learning how to write. The best way to learn something is to do it, and I took that idea and ran with it, pumping out book after book, learning bit by bit from complaints, bad reviews, sometimes nitpicking emails about the difference between a "clip" and a "magazine". But I also learned what people liked and learned to better tailor my stories to the flavors of contemporary readership, while not losing the voice that is distinctly mine. So, thank you to everyone who ever bought a book of mine and complained. You made me better.

The next step in my evolution came with the dreaded e-word—editing. I owe a huge thanks to my first editor who supports me in everything I do, and who will let me drag her around places when I feel anxious. In case you couldn't infer it, my first editor was my wife, and sharing my books with her was probably the most nerve-racking thing I'd ever done. Like, if you give your book to someone who loves you, and they tell you it's garbage, you know you're cooked. She bowed out somewhere around *The Enemies of Our Ancestors*. Some people are born to be editors and some are not. (She says she didn't like all the made-up names and it was hard to keep track of them.) But still, I owe her thanks. Who knows if I would have even written this book without her. When I woke up from the nightmare that inspired this book, I scribbled the details down in a notebook that has the words *Fucking Brilliant* emblazoned on the front . . . fitting for this book, I think. I'm still waiting for the next idea to put in that book.

From there, I enlisted the help of my friend Sahjo, who is really more comfortable reading fantasy, but she took a stab at editing my horror stuff, and pointed out a ton of annoying foibles I had. If it wasn't for her, there would be a thousand ellipses in this book. She still edits my *One Night Stand at the End of the World* series for me (that fantasy vibe), and always gives me valuable feedback. She's a great friend, but I think she's looking forward to the time when she can buy my books and read the finished product without having to pay attention to all my commas. Hope she enjoys this one.

From there, I jumped to Erin Al-Mehairi, who has edited a handful of my straight horror books, including the editing on this one before I ever sent it off to Matt and Alex at Tenebrous Press. Her insight has been invaluable and helped me unlock a new level in my writing. I can point to a clear delineation in my writing style, and I refer to this as my pre-Erin-phase and my post-Erin-phase. She rocks. Send her work. **WE LIKE IT CHERRY** came out of my head fully formed story-wise, but Erin helped me tame some of my artistry and style, which all artists need every now and then.

I have to thank Alex and Matt for having a cool press like Tenebrous in the first place. I've worked with a few presses now, and I can honestly say, they are my favorite. The respect and care they have shown for this work is top-notch. Even when I started getting choosy about cover designs, they didn't bat an eye. I'm extremely indebted to them for still opening the submissions I send them . . . because I have sent them some weird stuff . . . like really weird. (Check out those delicious ellipses.)

I also owe a big shout out to Carlos E. Rivera, author of the *White Harbor Trilogy* and a true friend. Reading his books gave me the confidence to write in a perspective not my own. I figured if Carlos could write straight characters as well as he writes queer characters, I ought to be able to do the same. Indeed, as an ally, I find it imperative that authors get out of our comfort zones and explore characters from all walks of life, always with an eye to respectful representation.

In addition to Carlos, I also owe a huge thanks to my Advanced Reading Crew, with special shout-outs to Karen H. and Michelle K. They always hit me with the feedback, and let me know when they liked something or didn't like it. Honest feedback is gold in this industry, and they were probably the first ones, along with other members of the crew, to put their eyes on **WE LIKE IT CHERRY** and let me know I really had something with this story. Thanks for the gold.

Finally, thanks to all my fans, which is something I never thought I would say when I first started writing. It takes a special brand of hubris to sit in front of a laptop for hours at a time, for weeks on end, and pretend the world will actually care about what you write. But they must, because I have actual fans! You all keep me going and lift my spirits when the grind of being a writer gets to me, which isn't too often, thanks to you. So thanks, and sorry for always killing your favorite characters.

Until the next one,

Jacy

ABOUT THE CONTRIBUTORS

Jacy Morris is a Native American author and a registered member of the Confederated Tribes of Siletz. At the age of ten he was transplanted to Portland, Oregon, where he developed a love for punk rock and horror movies, both of which tend to find their way into his writing. He has been an English and social studies teacher in Portland since 2005.

Blacky Shepherd is a Pacific Northwest-based artist and writer, best known for his Horror collaborations with Cullen Bunn. He's also done work on *G.I. Joe* and *Transformers* for IDW Comics, and is currently working on a boutique toy line based on his original characters.

A note on the cover art:
Designed by Tenebrous Editor-in-Chief **Alex Woodroe**, the original photo was taken from the public domain, and originally photographed by **Herbert Ponting**, entitled "British Antarctic (Terra Nova) Expedition—(1910-1913)."

CONTENT WARNINGS

Being a work of mature Horror, a degree of violence, gore, sex and/or death is to be expected.

In addition, *We Like It Cherry* contains scenes of:

Homophobia (language)

Wild Animal Death (off-page)

Animal Consumption (ceremonial)

Please be advised.

More information at
www.tenebrouspress.com

Grab another Tenebrous title!

Grab another Tenebrous title!

TENEBROUS

PRESS

Home of New Weird Horror, New Weird Dark Fiction, Oddities, Abnormalities and All Manner of Eccentricities You Never Knew You Needed More Than Oxygen

FIND OUT MORE:

www.tenebrouspress.com

@TenebrousPress on social media

HAIL THE TENEBROUS CULT

www.ingramcontent.com/pod-product-compliance
Lightning Source LLC
LaVergne TN
LVHW040544130625
813546LV00001B/8